"DO YOU THINK THE MAKEOVER CLUB COULD HELP LENA?"

"You forget," said Rissa, thinking back to her own pre-Makeover days, "I was pretty hopeless myself."

"I always liked you," Mike said. "I never saw a girl who could play a better game of basketball."

"You didn't *like* me, though," Rissa reminded him.

"Not like I *like* you now," Mike teased, taking her hand.

"That settles it," Rissa said after a few moments. "I'm calling an emergency meeting of the Makeover Club for this Saturday. Project Lena is about to begin."

Other Avon Flare Books by
Suzanne Weyn

THE MAKEOVER CLUB

THE MAKEOVER SUMMER

SUZANNE WEYN

AN AVON FLARE BOOK

For Ms. Mary Mohr,
who has been scheming, dreaming,
laughing and crying with me
since high school.
No one could ever have
a better friend.

Chapter One

This was going to be the best summer of their lives! That's what Marsha Kranton was thinking as she climbed into the backseat of Mike Meadows's beat-up blue Mustang. "I still can't believe we actually have summer jobs," she said.

"Thanks to Mike," added Marsha's friend, Rissa, turning around from the front seat where she sat between her boyfriend Mike and her brother Roger.

"What about me?" cried Roger. "I put in a good word for you too."

"Oh, Roger," Rissa replied, "I know you did. But face it. You just work in the pool locker room at Hemway Park. Mike is the head lifeguard again this year. I'm sure his opinion meant everything to Mr. Monahan when it came to hiring summer help."

"Hold on," laughed Mike, "I don't have that much pull with maniac Monahan. He just asked if I knew any kids who wanted part-time work this summer. So I gave him your names. If you guys hadn't had good interviews he wouldn't have hired you no matter what I said."

"Well, maybe," Rissa conceded. "All I know is that I couldn't have faced another summer as boring as last year's."

"A lot has changed since then," Marsha observed,

settling back in her seat, carefully avoiding the spots where the springs seemed ready to burst through the seat cover.

"Yeah, a lot," Rissa agreed, gently touching Mike's arm.

As the car traveled along Hillside Avenue toward their friend Sara Marshall's house—the last pickup on the way to Hemway Park—Marsha's mind wandered back to last summer. She, Rissa, and Sara had been three awkward eighth graders who were scared to death of starting high school. But their freshman year at Rosemont High hadn't been as bad as they'd feared. In fact, all things considered, it had turned out pretty well—thanks to the Makeover Club.

The Makeover Club was a club they had formed when they'd decided that with a little work they might come close to transforming themselves into the pretty, popular girls they'd dreamed of being. They'd exercised, experimented with makeup, hairstyles, and clothing. They tried anything that might make them look better. And it had worked. Rissa had won a one-year modeling contract with *Teen Today* magazine, and after years of being "just friends," she and Mike were now something more. Marsha had lost almost twenty pounds and was seeing a nice guy named Jim Connors. And Sara had begun singing with a local rock band and found—well, a style all her own.

Marsha looked at Rissa, whose soft, wavy blonde hair was cut into a sporty short cut. It seemed to Marsha that Rissa had changed the most. She'd even changed her name from Clarissa Lupinski to her "modeling name," Rissa Sky. The Rissa had stuck, the Sky hadn't. Rissa now settled for calling herself Rissa Lupinski.

Inside, Rissa wasn't totally different, though. "I'm

no longer a tomboy," she'd announced one day. "I'm a sportswoman." Marsha figured that was fair enough.

Marsha looked at her own reflection in the car window. Gone were the big thick glasses she'd worn last year and the twenty extra pounds. And gone was the stupid bowl haircut. She now saw a girl with green eyes, long brown hair caught up in a French braid, and a cute, if slightly pug, nose. She'd learned that she could be both smart and pretty. It felt good.

And then there was Sara. . . .

"Oh, no!" Rissa's voice shook Marsha from her reverie. "Take a look at this."

The car had pulled up in front of Sara's brick house. Sara ran across the lawn toward them. Her short, dyed orange hair stood up in little moussed spikes. The ever-present Walkman hung around her neck, and her wrists were loaded with bangle bracelets. She wore a particularly iridescent red lipstick. In sharp contrast to this she had on an orangish-brown, starched-stiff skirt and vest over a white short sleeved blouse. The Hemway Park uniform looked at least one size too big for her and the sleeves of the blouse stood straight out, making Sara's skinny arms look especially scarecrow-like.

Roger let out a low whistle as Sara approached. "Pretty sexy," he teased. "And I love those shoes," he added, indicating the flat brown Oxfords Sara wore.

Sara stopped and covered her face with her hands in embarrassment. When she took them away her eyes were crossed and her tongue was sticking out in an expression of ridiculous horror. "Do you *be-lieeeeve* this uniform!" she cried, climbing into the car beside Marsha. "All the girls who work in the parking lot have to wear the same thing. When I picked it up the other day I almost died. And I actually had to buy these shoes."

"I don't know which is weirder," Rissa scoffed,

3

"the uniform or your hair. You look like a spray-painted porcupine."

"I'm always on the cutting edge of fashion," Sara replied coolly, "even if I am stuck in this super-twerp uniform."

Marsha had to laugh. It was true: Some things hadn't changed at all. Sara and Rissa, the most loyal of friends, still bickered. Rissa never understood Sara's transition from a shy washed-out girl to a rock and roll firecracker with wild hair, bright makeup, and crazy clothes. But even Rissa had to admit that Sara had never seemed happier. She was singing with the band and going with—sort of—the band's leader, Nicky James. Sara and Nicky never really went out, but it was clear that they liked each other a lot.

The three friends had suspended Makeover Club meetings until the fall. There were just too many other things taking up their time lately. And the truth of it was, once they'd grown more confident about themselves they'd lost interest in the weekly meetings.

Sara hummed the latest of the group's songs. "You sure seem happy for someone stuck in that horrible outfit," Marsha observed.

"Nothing could make me unhappy this summer," Sara replied. "Elaine left yesterday for Switzerland. She's going to study opera for the whole summer."

Elaine was Sara's older sister, and two more opposite sisters never existed. "An entire summer without hearing her wailing away up in her room. Plus I get to wear all the clothes she didn't take with her—and she'll never know."

"I always wanted to see Switzerland," Mike said as he eased the car onto the highway. "Where's she staying?"

"With a family that my father knows in Zurich. They were supposed to send their fifteen-year-old

4

daughter here for the summer so she could take special English literature classes at the college, but she chickened out. So now I have the house totally to myself. It's heaven."

"I think it would be interesting to live with a foreign student for the summer," Marsha said. "It could be a lot of fun."

"No way," yelped Sara. "I'd be totally responsible for her. I'd have to drag her around with me everywhere."

"Maybe you wouldn't," said Rissa.

"Oh, yes I would. I can just hear my mother—'Sara, I don't think you're being very nice to our guest by always running out with your friends.' Yuck!"

"Well, she's not coming so you don't have to worry," said Marsha. An only child, Marsha often thought having a sister, or even someone just for the summer, would be nice company. But, she supposed, if you were always surrounded by sisters and brothers then being alone might look good to you.

Five minutes later the car pulled into the big parking lot. The girls felt very "in" driving through the special "Employees Only" gate. The morning sun glinted off the cement of the empty parking lot. Hemway was a new state park. It had a huge pool, tennis courts, picnic grounds, even a bandshell for concerts. This summer Sara would be collecting parking fees, Rissa had gotten a job as a junior lifeguard, and Marsha was going to work in the baby-sitting center.

"This is so exciting," said Marsha.

A few minutes after saying good-bye to her friends, Sara found herself standing outside a small white and green house that was the office of Mr. Meyer, the man in charge of the parking lot. Beside her stood a girl with long blonde hair that hung in big curls. She wore an orangish-brown uniform identical to Sara's except, Sara couldn't help but notice, hers fit.

"Hi," the girl said. "I'm Meredith Meyer. You can call me Merry. All my friends do."

"Sara Marshall. Nice to meet you," Sara replied. "Hey, you have the same last name as our boss."

"That's Daddy," Merry answered.

Just then Mr. Meyer walked briskly out of his office. "Come with me, ladies," he said. "I am about to give you a tour of our toll booths. I call them Gabriel and Michael because they remind me of two angels standing guard at the entranceway of Hemway Park."

"Ha! That's pretty funny," laughed Sara, assuming that Mr. Meyer was making a joke.

He didn't laugh. Instead he stared at Sara as if seeing her for the first time. "I must make something perfectly clear to you at the outset, Miss Marshall," he said sternly. "You are standing at the hub—the pumping heart—of Hemway Park. No parking fees mean no revenues. No revenues mean no park. Do not deceive yourself for one minute that taxes fully support Hemway. It's parking fees that are the life blood of—"

"Could we hear more about Michael and Gabriel, Daddy?" Merry interrupted, sounding as if she'd heard this speech before.

Mr. Meyer showed them how to work the machine that dispensed different colored parking tickets. There were orange tickets for the regular three-dollar fee. The blue tickets were for senior citizens, and the yellow were for local town residents with authorized stickers on their windshields. He showed them how he wanted the tickets counted and the money tallied at the end of their shift. "I expect ticket count and fees to match to the penny," he told them.

Sara looked at Merry, trying to tell if she was as

confused as Sara. But Merry just listened to her father adoringly and nodded her head, seeming to understand completely everything he said.

She's probably genetically predisposed to love taking parking fees, thought Sara despairingly. *My luck, I've wandered into a family of parking fee fanatics.*

Mr. Meyer assigned Sara to Michael and Merry to Gabriel. "I have to go pick up a delivery of tickets at the post office," he told them. "Traffic should be slow for another hour or so." He walked off a few paces and then turned back. "And remember to follow the rules as I've laid them out. No exceptions. I always say, rules are rules."

The booths were only a car-width apart and open at the sides. Sara could see Merry primping in her pocket mirror in the other booth.

"I guess you know all about this parking fee stuff, since it's in your family and all," Sara called over, making conversation.

"I feel like Michael and Gabriel *are* my family," Merry shouted back.

"You must understand how all these different colored tickets and the tally sheet and all works."

"No. I usually don't listen to Daddy when he starts talking about parking fees. It's so boring I just tune him out. I wasn't exactly sure what he was talking about today. I didn't even want this job. Daddy made me take it."

Just then the first car pulled into Sara's lane. Sara took the fee, made change, gave the ticket, and hit the number counter on the dispenser.

The next car also pulled into Sara's lane. Her eyes brightened when she saw who was in the black 1960 Corvair convertible.

"Hey, you Eggheads, totally def wheels," she shouted.

7

"My dad's," said Stingo, the drummer for Sara's rock group, Nicky and the Eggheads. Nicky sat beside Stingo. The other members, Tom and Eddie, were in the backseat.

"That's a totally def outfit," said Nicky.

Sara was suddenly self-conscious. "I have to wear this," she explained defensively.

"No, I'm serious," said Nicky, "It's so out it's in. You look wild in it."

"Yeah?" Sara beamed at him. No one made her feel as wonderful as Nicky did. She loved everything about him: his cute British accent (he'd come from London last year); his blond hair which he'd recently changed from a modified Mohawk to a short, blond flat-top; the single hoop earring he wore. Everything.

Even though they never actually went out on dates, Sara felt that she and Nicky shared something special. He always walked her home from rehearsals and sometimes he kissed her good night. They weren't long, passionate kisses—but they were kisses.

"We're going to take a swim," Nicky told her. "If you're ready to go by the time we leave we can give you a lift home. I'll come back and check in when we're about to go."

"Great," said Sara, handing Stingo his orange ticket. They drove through and Sara handled the next few cars pretty well. They were all coming into her lane since it was the one closest to the road. *This really isn't hard*, she told herself.

Soon a white Mercedes with an open sunroof pulled into her lane. At the wheel sat a boy Sara recognized as someone who had graduated from Rosemont that June. Beside him sat Doris Gaylord, the person Sara most despised in the world.

Sara had to admit that Doris looked good today, as she always did. She wore her long brown hair clipped up high on the sides and falling to her shoulders in flowing brown curls. Doris was very popular with the "right" crowd at Rosemont High. She was rich, gorgeous, and incredibly snotty. Sara, Marsha, and Rissa had all locked horns with Doris in one way or another and now they had a running feud. In the seat behind Doris sat Doris's friends Heather Irving and Craig Lawrence.

"My, my," crooned Doris, leaning over the driver toward the open window, "Isn't it nice of Hemway to hire the mentally weird."

"Always nauseating to see you too, Doris." Another car pulled into the lane behind the Mercedes. "Three dollars, please," Sara requested, eager to be rid of Doris and her friends.

The boy at the wheel reached into his pocket, but Doris stopped him. "I insist on paying," she said with a malicious gleam in her eye. She pulled out a small tapestry change purse. "Let's see, I have a quarter and a dime . . . that's thirty-five cents. Here's another dime. That's forty-five . . ."

Sara saw that another car was coming in. Luckily it pulled into Merry's lane. Doris stuck a handful of change out the window to Sara. "There, that's a dollar," she said. "Anyone else got change?" she asked her friends, who snickered and rummaged through their pockets.

Sara noticed that Merry's lane was accumulating a long lineup of cars. She looked over and saw that Merry seemed to be having trouble with an elderly woman in a big car. "Ma'am, it doesn't matter if you're going to be sixty in August, you don't qualify as a senior citizen until then. I'm sorry, rules are rules," Sara heard her tell the woman.

"A dollar seventy-five," said Doris, handing more change out the window.

9

The line of cars was now backed up out to the street. Sara ran over to Merry's booth. "Here," she said, taking the woman's two dollars and handing her a blue ticket. "Have a nice day."

"Daddy would kill me for that," said Merry nervously. "He always says rules are rules."

"We have a traffic jam here," Sara shouted. A car out on the road blared its horn. Then another and another.

"This makes me so nervous," whimpered Merry. "And when I'm nervous I have to go to the bathroom."

Sara smiled. "I know what you mean," she said. "I always get the hiccups when I'm nervous."

Merry wasn't listening to Sara. She was hopping up and down and grabbing her purse. "Cover for me while I run to the little girls' room."

"Cover for—" It was no use. Merry trotted off toward the ladies' room in the main building. The sound of horns was now almost deafening.

Sara ran back to the white Mercedes. "Two-seventy-five," Doris said laughingly as she handed more change through the car window.

"Good enough," said Sara, dropping an orange ticket into the window. "Go!"

Finally, they drove off. In the next car was a man who claimed he was entitled to town rates even though he didn't have a sticker.

"Fine," said Sara, handing him a yellow ticket. She ran back to Merry's booth only to find a woman who needed change for a hundred dollar bill. "Forget it," Sara told her. "There's free parking today. Go right through." People were getting out of their cars to see what was causing the delay.

This was ridiculous. Sara had to do something! She stood between the two car lanes and waved the cars in.

10

"Free parking for the first fifteen cars!" she shouted. "Free . . . hic . . . hic . . . parking. Special opening day . . . hic . . . discount for the . . . hic . . ."

The honking stopped as the cars flowed into the lot. Sara counted fifteen cars and then prepared to tell the sixteenth that the regular rates were back in effect. She approached the sixteenth car as it pulled up to the booth.

"What is going on here?" shouted Mr. Meyer, in the sixteenth car. "And what happened to Merry?"

"I . . . hic, uh . . . she went to the . . . hic . . . bathroom."

"My first day of work and I'm already on probation," moaned Sara. She was sitting next to Nicky on the bench by the main building.

He put his arm around her and squeezed. "Come on, we're ready to leave. We'll drop you home."

Sara got up and walked toward the phone booth. "Thanks. I'll call my mother and tell her she doesn't have to pick me up."

"Want to go over some new songs tonight?" Nicky asked.

"No. I hope you don't mind, but I'm beat. I've had enough excitement for one day. The way I feel now, I could live without excitement for the rest of my life."

Sara's mother answered the phone. "Sara, dear," she said. "I can't wait for you to get home. I have the most exciting news!"

Chapter Two

The next day Sara wasn't scheduled to work. Rissa and Marsha stood together outside the lifeguard station of the Hemway pool. Rissa looked neat and official in her green tank suit, blue shorts, and white sandals. She was blowing softly on the whistle she wore on a cord around her neck.

Both girls had arrived early. Rissa was waiting to help a senior lifeguard conduct a tadpole class for three- and four-year-olds in the baby pool. Marsha was waiting for the baby-sitting center to open at nine o'clock.

"I wonder what's with Sara," Marsha said. "I called her last night. She said she couldn't talk but that her summer was totally ruined. She sounded really upset."

"Sara always dramatizes everything," said Rissa, shaking the whistle to find out why it had stopped making a sound.

"I know, but this seemed serious. She told me she'd try to come to the park today if she could."

Marsha looked at the clock on the wall. "Only ten more minutes till Tot Terror! I hope there aren't as many kids today as yesterday. I was so beat when I got home that I fell asleep at eight-thirty."

"I tried to get to sleep early, but my dear, darling

younger brother Fred kept blasting his new Iron Maiden tape over and over. Roger threatened to break his boom box, so Fred locked the door and wouldn't let anyone in. No one could get him to stop."

"What did your father do?"

"Are you ready for this?" Rissa said, leaning in close, "Pete was out on a date."

Marsha's jaw dropped open. "No!"

"I swear."

Marsha could not picture Rissa's gruff, stern father on a date. Ever since Rissa's mother had died when Rissa was six, her father had raised Rissa and her four brothers as if they were all boys. Her house was a jumble of baseball gloves, hockey skates, car parts, skateboards, fishing poles, and greasy fingerprints. Rissa often felt there was no place for her feminine side in her house. Life there revolved around sports and car engines.

"What's the woman like?" Marsha asked.

"We've never met her, but knowing Dad, she's probably a lady sumo wrestler."

"Give ol' Pete some credit," Marsha laughed. "He did marry your mother, after all." Marsha looked at the clock again. "It's almost nine. Gotta go!"

The baby-sitting center was already hopping when Marsha got there. Most of the kids at the center were between two and four. They were sweet—most of the time—and they kept things moving at a frantic pace. If the day passed like it had yesterday, Marsha wouldn't have a moment to be bored. There was always a question to be answered, a boo-boo to be kissed, a stray child to be brought gently back into the group, a nose to be wiped, a frightened child to be soothed. It made Marsha feel frazzled but happy.

After Marsha left, Rissa hung around the lifeguards' office waiting for the tadpole swimming class to begin.

She looked at herself in the mirror of the first-aid cabinet, feeling very in charge in her lifeguard's tank suit. The bossy part of Rissa's personality delighted in telling people what to do. "Don't run. No food in the swimming area. No bare feet allowed." And the part of her that truly loved being part of a team enjoyed the way the lifeguards assisted one another in giving lessons, covering shifts, and doing the general pool chores.

"Ready to teach those little tadpoles to blow bubbles?" Mike walked into the office and picked up a clipboard from the desk.

"Am I assisting you?" Rissa asked happily.

"Yep," he answered, giving her the broad smile she loved. "I made up all the assisting assignments. You may not be so happy once you finish helping me with this class. When those little kids get water up their noses, they freak."

"I don't care. This is great!" she answered, giving her whistle cord an exuberant twirl. She loved working with Mike. She thought he looked even more handsome than usual in his green trunks with the official white Hemway Park polo shirt over them. As far as Rissa was concerned, being Mike's girlfriend was the best thing that had ever happened to her—maybe even better than winning the *Teen Today* modeling contract. After years of being buddies, Mike and Rissa were close friends. The romance part just made it doubly wonderful being near him. His brown curly hair, his blue eyes, his ambling athletic walk, even his peeling sunburn—she thought everything about him was just perfect.

They walked together over to the baby pool where three little boys and two little girls sat on the edge of the pool with their feet in the water. Their proud and anxious mothers hovered nearby.

Rissa waded into the shallow water, while Mike took down names and numbers from the mothers. Rissa gave her whistle a soft toot. "Okay, tadpoles, we're going to teach you how to swim like big strong frogs," she said. "Can you say *ribbit* like a frog?"

First there was one soft *ribbit*. Then another.

"Good!" shouted Rissa. "Now let's all *ribbit* and make a big splash with our feet."

Ribbit! Ribbit! Ribbit! The pool was filled with the sound of splashing and frog croaks. It suddenly occurred to Rissa that she should have waited for Mike. She looked at him with a questioning expression, but he just smiled and gave her the thumbs-up sign.

By three o'clock both Marsha and Rissa were done with their shifts. Marsha was waiting for Rissa to finish changing in the locker room when Sara came rushing in. "Thank God you guys haven't left yet!" she cried, running over to Marsha.

"We were going to take the bus home."

"You can't. You have to stay here with me. You have to."

"Sara, would you please tell me what's going on."

"It's her. Lena Laffleberger. She's here. This is so awful!"

"Lena what?" asked Marsha, starting to think her friend had a touch of sunstroke from the day before.

"Laffleberger! Laffleberger!" shouted Sara, as if the answer should have been perfectly obvious. "The foreign exchange student! She's come all the way from Switzerland to destroy my life!"

"I thought she'd decided not to come," said Rissa.

"She just changed her mind again and her parents booked her on the first flight that had a cancellation."

"Can she speak English?" Marsha asked.

"Her English is fine. As a matter of fact, she also speaks German, Italian, and French. That's why she's

15

taking the special classes at the college—because she was tops in her class in English.''

"This is not exactly a tragedy, Sara,'' Rissa pointed out as she leaned forward to towel dry her short blonde hair.

"You don't think so? Wait until you—''

Just then a tall, heavyset girl with wispy, shoulder length blonde hair walked into the locker room and looked around.

"That's her,'' whispered Sara, who had ducked behind Rissa. "My mother said I had to bring her here with me. I told you I'd have to drag her everywhere.''

"Whew,'' whispered Rissa. "She's a big one.'' The girl was at least five feet, ten inches tall and had to weigh close to 160 pounds. She wasn't so much fat as she was just BIG.

"Is she nice?'' Marsha whispered.

Sara whispered back, "She's just sort of—strange. You'll see.''

The girl caught sight of Sara and waved. The three friends waved back feebly as the girl approached them. "Ah, there you are,'' she said in a thick accent. "I was thinking that I had lost you in this crowd.''

"Oh, um, no, no, I was just talking to my friends,'' sputtered Sara. "Lena, this is Rissa Lupinski and Marsha Kranton. They're my two very, *very* best friends, who *never* leave my side when I *need them desperately.*'' Sara added the last part while staring at Marsha and Rissa meaningfully.

Lena stuck her hand out and shook both Marsha's and Rissa's hands vigorously. Up close, the girls saw that Lena had pale white skin. Blonde lashes and eyebrows framed a pair of China-blue eyes. Her thickish pink lips seemed too big for the rest of her face. A pale line of freckles sprayed across her rather flat nose.

"You are a cute munchkin," Lena said to Marsha.

"I beg your pardon?" Marsha replied.

"A munchkin, that's good," Lena went on. She then broke into a laugh that was more like a series of loud snorts.

Baffled, Marsha turned to her friends for help. "I think she noticed that you're kind of short," Sara told her.

"Oh, well," Marsha stuttered. She'd always been sensitive about her height. Her mother had suggested that since she was only fifteen she might still gain a few more inches before she stopped growing, but Marsha hadn't grown much in the last year. It was pretty clear to her that she would always be only five feet tall.

Marsha knew she was short, but she certainly didn't like some stranger making jokes about it. She wanted to shout back, "Overgrown clod!" but she simply found herself turning red.

"It is fine to be a munchkin," said Lena, "It is very cute."

"Yeah, well I don't want to be cute," Marsha muttered.

"You should not worry," Lena continued. "It is better to be cute than to be a giant like me. Your friend Rissa knows what I mean about being a giant."

"Look, Lena," said Sara, trying to stop the beginning of an argument, "why don't you change into your suit and wait for us by the pool, okay?"

"Okay," Lena agreed, smiling.

"Fine, see you outside," Sara replied, waving Lena over toward one of the dressing booths.

"How long is she staying?" Marsha asked when Lena was out of earshot.

"The whole summer. The whole summer," Sara whimpered. "*Now* do you see what I mean?"

"It's been nice knowing you, Sara," Rissa said dryly. "You're on your own on this one."

"Oh, no!" shouted Sara. "I stick with you when you have problems. No way are you leaving me stuck with her."

"Hang on," Marsha cut in, "maybe she's just scared."

Lena stood outside the ladies' locker room and waited, looking down the cement ramp that led from the area outside the locker room to the pool. Running her hand across her stomach she tried to ease the butterflies that seemed to be flapping their wings madly inside her. She had the uneasy feeling that her first meeting with Sara's friends hadn't gone well. She was just trying to be friendly, to make conversation. Lena sighed. It was a strain making conversation with so many new people. And she worried that maybe she hadn't used exactly the right English words.

Lena saw Sara, Marsha, and Rissa walking out the short tunnel that led from the locker room. This was her chance to start fresh. She'd try even harder to make them like her.

"Hurry," she said to them happily. "Let us get into the water before people see us in our bathing suits and start to laugh."

Marsha didn't get home until six o'clock. Sara hadn't let Marsha and Rissa leave her side. Wearily she plopped down on the couch. She heard her mother in the kitchen. It was strange for her mother to be home all day. Mrs. Kranton taught at the local college and usually didn't get home until six, but she'd decided not to teach this summer.

"Rough day?" asked her mother, coming into the

18

living room. She sat down on the loveseat across from Marsha and wiped her glasses on her shirt.

"Work wasn't so bad, just lots of screaming kids," Marsha said. "The hard part was putting up with the girl from Switzerland who's visiting the Marshalls for the summer. Wow, is she awful!"

"What's so bad about her?"

"For one thing she's big as a house."

"Now Marsha, that's not—"

"That's not what's wrong with her, Mom. She's got a total case of foot-in-mouth disease. The first thing she said to me was that I was a munchkin. Then she called Rissa a giant and implied that we all looked laughable in out bathing suits. Down at the pool she met Mike and she told him that his sunburn made him look like a red zebra. She started calling Nicky Mr. Potato Head because his hair is so short . . ."

Marsha's mother stifled a laugh.

"It's not funny," Marsha said, though she laughed in spite of herself. "We're stuck with her for the whole summer. Doris Gaylord has already started making loud cracks about her. She kept saying 'Geese of a feather honk together,' and that stupid Heather Irving kept making goose noises every time we walked by. It was mortifying."

"Now Marsha," her mother said with a knowing smile that Marsha found annoying, "I thought you'd learned to just tune those girls out."

"She has a point though," Marsha protested. "If we have to hang out with her then we'll look like geeks by association. This girl is horrible. Do you know what she said to Jim when she met him? She said he looked like an elf and that he reminded her of one of Santa's helpers."

"He does have a certain pixie's gleam in his eyes."

"Mother!"

"Okay, okay. It does sound like someone should give her a few lessons in tact. Speaking of Jim, he called just a few minutes before you walked in. He wants you to call him."

"Thanks." Marsha's mother returned to the kitchen and Marsha stretched out on the couch. She wondered why she didn't want to jump up right away to call Jim back. It had been bothering her a lot, this lukewarm feeling she had toward him. He was certainly a perfectly nice boyfriend. They had been partners in the debate club and had won a tournament together. She'd asked him to the June dance and they'd been going together ever since then, almost three weeks now. He was cute and funny, and she knew he liked her a lot. It seemed to her she should be happy.

It was just that Marsha had always dreamed that her first romance would be something that swept her away with excitement. Her feeling toward Craig Lawrence last year had been closer to what she had in mind. Even though Craig turned out to be a real creep, her heart had raced whenever he came near her. With Jim she felt a warm, friendly feeling. Sometimes it seemed as if Jim were her brother rather than her boyfriend. *Oh, well,* she thought, *it's all in my head. I'm lucky to find a boy as nice as Jim. And we have fun together, so there's not really anything to complain about.*

When she returned Jim's call, the first thing he said was, "Hi. Ready for Freddy?"

"What? Oh, I almost forgot, sure." Marsha had forgotten that tonight Jim was holding a *Nightmare on Elm Street* festival. He'd rented all the *Nightmare on Elm Street* movies (he'd had to reserve them over a month ago) and he planned to show them on his family's extra-wide-screen TV. Marsha wasn't crazy about horror movies but they always had fun when Jim had his at-home film festivals. He invited lots of kids

20

over and they'd spend more time throwing popcorn at each other and shouting wisecracks at the screen than actually watching the movie.

"I called Sara to invite her but she said she couldn't come, and something about never being able to show her face in public again?"

"She doesn't want to give Lena the chance to insult any more people," Marsha explained.

Jim laughed. "She's some piece of work, that Lena."

"I feel sorry for Sara having to live with her," Marsha commented. "Listen, did you remind Rissa, Mike, and Roger that it's Freddy night?"

"Not yet."

"I'll call Rissa. What time?"

"Freddy appears at seven. Come over earlier if you can."

Marsha was about to call Rissa when the phone rang. It was Rissa. "Hi," said Marsha, "I was just going to call to tell you that—"

"Listen to this," Rissa cut her off excitedly. "*Teen Today* phoned and they want me to audition for a TV commercial to promote the magazine. Me on TV! I could never do it. I'd be too nervous."

"Sure you can," Marsha assured her. "You didn't think you could win the *Teen Today* contest and you did."

"I have to be there this Thursday. I'll have to get some time off from work. I hope Mike will give it to me."

"Sure he will," said Marsha.

"He probably will, but he'll be crabby about it. Any time I mention anything about modeling he goes all moody on me."

"That's strange," said Marsha. "He's usually not like that."

21

"I know. He told me once that he's afraid that if I become a famous model I won't be interested in him anymore. What a strange idea. But he really worries about it. Anyway, do you guys want to come to the city with me?"

"Sara and I both have off this Thursday, but Sara will be stuck with Lena."

"Oh, I guess she can come too," Rissa said grouchily, after a few moments hesitation.

"She's not mean, just weird, that's all," said Marsha, trying to be charitable. "Speaking of weird, are you ready for Freddy Night at Jim's?"

Rissa just cackled evilly over the phone.

"I guess that means yes," said Marsha. "See you around seven."

That evening Sara sat glumly next to Lena on the plaid couch in the family den, listening as Lena snorted merrily at everything on TV. Somehow nothing struck Sara as being funny.

Sara's mother and father seemed especially kindly and perky tonight, as if they were trying to imitate TV parents, who were always patient and intensely interested in everything their kids did. Even the way they were sitting bugged Sara. Their posture seemed a little too straight and perfect.

"So, Lena, how did you enjoy your first full day in the United States?" asked Mr. Marshall.

"It was the best!" Lena answered enthusiastically. "Sara has very nice friends, and they were all so kind to me. I hope the students at the college are equally friendly."

"I'm sure they will be," Sara's mother assured Lena. "Did you have a good time today, Sara?"

"It was too marvelous for words," Sara replied sarcastically. Her mother shot Sara a warning glance.

"I'm pretty tired and I don't feel so well," Sara lied. "I think I'll say good night."

Up in her room, Sara lay on her bed listening to her Walkman. Lena was going to drive her crazy. Even Marsha and Rissa weren't going to want to hang out with her anymore—and who could blame them! Every time Lena opened her mouth she said something that rubbed someone the wrong way. And Nicky! How long was he going to put up with her if she had to drag around this giant shadow who kept calling him Mr. Potato Head?

Sara fell asleep on top of her bedspread. She awoke to the sound of the door opening. She looked up and saw Lena standing in the bedroom doorway.

"What's happening?" Sara asked groggily. Her clock radio read twelve-fifteen.

"Your mother and father went to sleep at ten, but I cannot sleep," said Lena.

"Count sheep."

"I don't understand. Is this an American custom?"

"No, it's just an expression. You just visualize these sheep and you sort of see them in your head and picture them leaping over a fence or something and then you start counting how many and it's supposed to be really dull . . ." Sara could see Lena was perplexed. "Never mind."

"Do you think I could sleep in here with you? At home I always share a room with my younger sister Frieda."

"There's only one bed in here," Sara protested.

"I have my mattress right here," Lena said, stepping back into the hall and dragging in the mattress from Elaine's bed.

Lena pushed the mattress over so that it fell to the floor. She went back out into the hall and came back carrying her pillow and sheets.

Sara got up and changed into the oversized T-shirt she usually slept in. She looked at Lena in her man-tailored pajamas. Sara's hard heart melted just a little—Lena looked so lost standing there in her pj's.

Sara settled into bed and clicked off the lamp that swung out from the wall. "How come you changed your mind about coming here?" she asked in the dark.

"I was scared to come. I felt shy. But Mother and Father kept . . . how would you say it . . . strongly urging . . ."

"Nagging," Sara supplied the word.

"Yes, nagging me to come. They say it will make me less shy around people."

"You sure don't seem shy," commented Sara.

"No? Good. I tried very hard to be friendly and open with your friends. My mother says to just be myself and say what I think and everyone will like me fine."

"You were quite open with your thoughts today," said Sara.

"Not too open I hope."

"No, um . . . you were fine," Sara lied. "But I think you should stop calling Nicky Mr. Potato Head. He's sort of sensitive."

"I was just making a joke, but if you say so, I will stop."

Sara felt herself drifting off to sleep. "Good night," she said, yawning deeply.

"Good night, Sara."

It seemed to Sara that she'd only been asleep a few minutes when she was awakened by the sound of soft crying.

"You okay?" she asked gently.

"Okay, yes," came Lena's quivering reply. "I am sorry to have awakened you. I am fine."

"Are you sure?"

"Yes, sure."

"Okay. Good night."

Sara lay back in the darkness. Her eyes were filled with tears. She wasn't sure why, but whenever someone else cried, she started to cry too.

Sara was drifting back to sleep when she heard the muffled crying again. She slid off her bed and sat next to Lena who continued to whimper into her pillow.

"I say stupid, stupid things," Lena mumbled, still face down. "Everything I say comes out wrong, wrong, wrong."

"Maybe you're trying too hard," Sara suggested.

Lena turned around and looked at Sara with tear-filled eyes. "How do you not try to be friendly when you want everyone to like you so much?"

"I don't know, Lena," Sara admitted. "Just try to relax."

Lena wiped her eyes with the bottom of her pajama top. "Tomorrow I will not try so hard."

Sara gave Lena an encouraging squeeze. Lena settled back under her sheet. In minutes she was asleep.

Sara lay in bed berating herself for not being more sensitive to Lena. Of course the girl was homesick and felt out of place, and all Sara could think of was her own feelings. She told herself that tomorrow she would try harder to be nice to Lena.

She was almost asleep when once again Sara was awakened. This time it was by the sound of loud snoring—Lena's snoring. Yes, thought Sara, flipping over on her stomach and pulling her pillow over her head—tomorrow she would have to try very hard.

Chapter Three

Rissa rose early on Thursday. She stood at her window and noticed the way the morning sun glinted off the leaves of the big tree in the backyard. She felt a hard knot form in her stomach. She was terrified of going on this audition, but she couldn't let that stop her. She had to go.

She went into the bathroom and stood under the shower. She was already in the habit of working at Hemway and it felt strange not to be going there this morning. Mike had arranged for someone else to take her shift, but, as she'd predicted, he hadn't done it graciously. Why couldn't he see how much this chance at a modeling career meant to her? It would never change how she felt about him. Right now, Mike was the most important person in her life. It seemed overly dramatic to use the word love to describe her feelings for him. But that's how she felt. She loved him.

Whether she loved him or not, Mike had to understand that modeling was her only chance to have a more glamorous life than the one she shared with her father and brothers. Not that things there were so bad—she knew her father worked hard to provide all they really needed. It was just that as she got older it all began to seem so ungracious and rough. She didn't want to end up in a house crammed full of sports equipment and broken-down cars always being tinkered with in the driveway.

No. Rissa wanted to travel, to have nice things, to meet exciting people. She was always a little embarrassed about these feelings. For one thing, she wasn't sure if they weren't just crazy dreams. And for another, they made her feel guilty, as if she were betraying her father and the life he'd made for her. Come to think of it, she even felt she was betraying her father sometimes simply by being a girl. It wasn't until lately, because she'd insisted on it, that he acknowledged she was female at all.

One person she never felt she was betraying was Mike. No matter how exotic her daydreams became—shooting photos in safari clothes in Africa, modeling kimonos in Japan—her dreams always included Mike. She was never sure exactly what he was doing there, but he was always beside her.

She towel dried her hair and slipped back into her robe. She rapped on her father's door. "Dad, it's almost six. Remember, you said you'd drive me to the city." A low grunt told her that he was up.

She set her hair in heated flexible bender rods that gave it a tousled look. She was glad she'd already gotten a light tan. It seemed to cover the few blemishes she had and it made her blue eyes appear even more vivid. A touch of gray eyeshadow in the creases of her eyelids, some mascara, a little blush on her high cheekbones, and a tinted lip gloss were all the makeup she wore.

She put on a light blue cotton drop-waist dress with short sleeves and full, gathered skirt. She liked this dress because as dresses went it was cool and comfortable.

She undid her rollers and pulled the curls out with her fingers. She studied herself in the half mirror above her dresser. *Not bad,* she thought.

When she got downstairs her father stood at the door

27

ready to go. Rissa gulped down a glass of milk and ran out behind him, still holding the donut she'd grabbed from the kitchen counter.

She climbed into her father's old Chevy. She hated being stuck alone with him during any season when she wasn't involved with team sports. Without sports it seemed as if they had nothing to talk about.

"Who's first?" he asked.

"Marsha."

They drove toward Marsha's in silence. "How was your date?" Rissa asked, searching for a topic of conversation. "Last night was your third one, wasn't it?"

"Was it?" her father replied absently.

"When are we going to meet this mystery woman?"

"I'm, uh, not sure. So, does the pool sponsor any swim meets?"

Rissa's father picked up Marsha, Sara, and Lena. The traffic moved quickly at that hour of the morning, but the girls were amazed at how many cars were already on the road and heading toward the city. Pete Lupinski drove through the tunnel and headed uptown. He dropped the girls off at a building near Rockefeller Center. By seven-thirty, the city was already awhirl with activity.

"I love Manhattan," Sara shouted. "I'm going to live here as soon as possible."

"Not me," said Rissa. "Too many weirdos."

"Zurich is nothing like this," said Lena, her face revealing how impressed she was with the city. "We have tall buildings and traffic, yes. But this is so big." Lena twirled around, trying to drink in all the sights of the city, and for a moment Sara felt her excitement. It must be such a thrill to see New York City for the first time.

Rissa showed the letter she'd received from *Teen*

Today to the security guard in the lobby. "Are all of you expected?" he asked.

"Yes, we're her assistants," Sara informed him. The guard raised his eyebrow at her, but let them pass.

The elevator opened onto the fifteenth floor. They walked down a dingy hall until they came to studio B, where Rissa had been told to report. Rissa cracked open the heavy door and the four girls peeked into a large, messy room. It was filled with movie cameras, harsh lights on poles, and folding chairs, and the floor was crisscrossed with cables. In the far end of the room stood two shallow stage sets. One set was a bright, clean, kitchen, the other was an elegant living room.

"Look, look," Sara grabbed Marsha's arm. "Don't you recognize that living room?"

Marsha stared at it. "No."

"Sure you do! That's Jessica Lane's living room. She moved there from the carriage house when she remarried Malcolm."

"Malcolm?"

"Her third husband who was kidnapped by the prince of Mondongo!"

"You're right." Marsha realized they were looking at a set from *The Young Searchers*, a daytime soap.

"And there she is!" Sara pointed out in an excited whisper.

Sure enough, Simone Martin, the actress who played Jessica Lane stepped out onto the set and spoke to a man who seemed to be the director. "I can't believe it! I love her!" cried Sara.

The girls entered the studio and were immediately intercepted by a young man holding a clipboard. "Can I help you?" he asked.

"I'm here for the *Teen Today* commercial," Rissa told him in a small voice.

"Go over there with the other girls," he said, nodding

his head toward a bunch of folding chairs in the far corner of the room where five pretty girls sat, each intently reading her script. "You'll be reading against Ms. Martin, who will be starring in the commercial."

"Simone Martin in your commercial!" squealed Sara.

"Are you girls also here for the audition?" the man asked.

"Oh, no, not us," Marsha answered backing away nervously. She remembered how she'd gotten involved in Rissa's *Teen Today* makeover simply by standing too close. She was definitely staying out of this event.

"You'll have to wait outside, then," the man told them.

"Oh, please, please, please, let us watch," Sara begged. "We'll sit over there in the corner and we won't make a sound."

The young man looked over his shoulder at the director who was busy walking around the stage with Simone Martin. "Not a peep out of you," he warned.

"Not even a whisper," Sara agreed.

"Okay, then sit over there and be quiet."

Rissa followed the man over to where the other girls were sitting. She sat down and began studying the script the man had handed her.

In a few minutes, the lights were aimed at the living room set. Simone Martin walked into the brightly lit area. She gazed at the camera and broke into the dazzling smile that was her trademark. "Today's teenage girls want to know what's hot and what's not," she read from the script in her hand. "They want the latest news on fashion, dating, fitness, and the world around them."

"Fine, Simone," said the director. He then pointed to a girl with long blonde hair. "You'll be girl one," he said, and, pointing to Rissa, "you'll be girl two. I want both of you to go up there next to Simone and read your parts."

The blonde girl stepped up to Simone Martin and read from her script, "But where can I find all that information, Simone?"

Simone then went into her spiel about how it was all in *Teen Today*. Rissa was next. "Excuse me," she said, stepping forward and shading her eyes from the bright lights. "It says here to do a little dance and cock my head to the right after I finish. What does that mean?"

"It means you're a perky, vibrant, modern teen," the director told her.

"It does? What kind of a dance do you want?"

"Be creative, give me something that shows that you're today, vibrant."

Marsha and Sara sunk down into their folding chairs and folded their arms at the same time. This worried them. They couldn't picture Rissa being perky.

"*Eeeewwww*, Simone, it's great to be a teen today," Rissa read flatly.

"Hold it dear," the director interrupted. "That *eeewwww* is supposed to be a squeal of delight. You made it sound like you'd just smelled something rotten. Try it again and give it all you've got. And let me see you dance with excitement this time."

"*Eeeeeeeeahhhhhhheeeewwwwwwww!*" Rissa trilled shrilly. "It's *grrrrreat* to be a teen today!" She then twirled around flinging her arms wildly and kicking her legs out.

The sight was so ridiculous that Marsha instinctively covered her eyes in embarrassment. Sara studied her shoes.

And Lena snorted with laughter. And snorted again . . . and again. She snorted and laughed and snorted. She was completely out of control.

"Yes it is great . . ." Simone Martin tried to read her lines, but her shoulders were shaking with sup-

31

pressed laughter. Apparently Rissa's dance and Lena's snorting were too much for her.

"Yes, it is gr . . ." she tried again. This time she collapsed laughing. The entire crew, the other girls, the man with the clipboard, and even the director, joined her.

The more laughter filled the room, the more contagious it was. Even Marsha and Sara had to cover their mouths to hold in giggles. The laughing spurred Lena on to louder snorts, and the more she snorted, the more everyone laughed.

Rissa just stood on stage smiling feebly, not sure whether to run away, or join the laughing.

"This is terrible," Marsha said breathlessly, trying to wipe the tears of laughter from her eyes. "Poor Rissa."

"Come on Rissa, talk to us," Marsha begged. "What happened wasn't our fault."

The girls were sitting in four seats at the front of the train bound for home. Rissa hadn't spoken to any of them all the way from the studio to Penn Station.

"I saw you," Rissa hissed. "You were laughing along with everyone else."

"We didn't start it," Sara said defensively. "Simone Martin did."

"Simone Martin would have controlled herself if *someone else* hadn't found my performance so hysterical." Rissa's last remark was aimed at Lena.

Lena hung her head. "Rissa, I cannot apologize enough. I thought your little jig was supposed to be, you know, what is the word . . . ?"

"Stupid, humiliating, ridiculous," Rissa offered.

"No, no, funny, humorous."

"Well, it wasn't. It was supposed to be cute, adorable, vivacious."

"It wasn't fair," Marsha pointed out. "They didn't

give you any practice. The other girl didn't have to do some dumb dance.''

"Yeah," Sara joined in, "and that director should have given you another chance, not just said, 'we'll call you,' after everyone stopped laughing. That wasn't very nice."

The rest of the trip was a silent and sullen one. Lena looked out the train window and watched the scenery rush by. She felt very far from home—and totally miserable. She'd been so happy this morning, so excited to have been invited along on this great adventure into Manhattan. And then she'd ruined it. She *had* thought that Rissa's dance was supposed to be funny. *Wrong again,* she told herself. *Wrong! Wrong! Wrong, as usual.* She bit her lip to keep from crying and wished she were home.

The train pulled into the Rosemont station at three o'clock. "It's really a scorcher today," observed Marsha. "Maybe I can convince my mother to drive us to Hemway for a swim."

"Good idea," said Sara.

"Yes, good," Lena agreed, grateful for anything that would lessen the tension she felt she'd caused.

Rissa just stood there silently. "Not me," she said after a few minutes. "I'm just going to go home and wish I was never born."

"Don't be like that," Marsha coaxed.

"I'll be however I want to be," replied Rissa, folding her arms.

Chapter Four

That afternoon, the temperature was over ninety degrees, so the Hemway pool was packed with people. Marsha and Sara stood outside the ladies' locker room waiting for Lena.

"Lena really feels badly about what happened," said Marsha. "It wasn't actually her fault. She can't help it if she has that stupid laugh."

"She wouldn't be so bad if someone would tape her mouth shut," offered Sara. "Every time she opens it there's more trouble."

A glum Lena emerged from the locker room. "God, that bright pink bathing suit makes her look huge," whispered Sara.

"Shhh," Marsha shushed her. Marsha always battled to keep her weight down and she was sensitive to any remarks, even if they were about someone else's weight.

They walked down to the main pool area where they met Mike, who was standing by one of the tall lifeguard's chairs. "Rissa with you?" he asked. He looked worried when they told him she hadn't felt like coming along. "Did the audition go badly?" he asked astutely.

"You could say that," Sara replied.

Just then a tall, blond lifeguard who was sitting in

34

the chair asked Mike when he could take his break. It was Tad Baker, an upperclassman Sara and Marsha recognized from Rosemont High. Sara and Marsha looked him over. He was gorgeous.

"Yoo, hoo, Tad," came an all-too-familiar voice. Doris pulled herself up out of the pool. She wore a very brief cranberry red bikini. Sara and Marsha looked at each other. Their glance said it all: They had to admit, however grudgingly, that the suit looked terrific on her.

"When are you going to give this boy a break, Mike?" she asked in the syrupy sweet voice she reserved exclusively for males of the species. "He's promised to give me a swimming lesson. I almost drowned last year at our house at the lake."

"Almost is such a disappointing word, Doris," said Sara acidly. "You should have tried harder."

"Do I hear an annoying buzz?" replied Doris. She turned her attention back to Tad. "So, Tad," she continued sweetly, "I hope you're getting off soon. I'm getting burned in this hot sun." As she spoke, Doris rubbed her nose to indicate her sunburn.

"Do not rub your nose," advised Lena urgently.

"What's your problem?" Doris asked Lena.

"You are rubbing the makeup off that red bump at the end of your nose," Lena told her in a whisper so loud everyone could hear it.

What Lena had said was true. Forgetting it was there, Doris had rubbed her waterproof cover-up makeup and a fairly small red blemish shone through.

"That's a real honker of a zit you've got there, Doris," said Sara.

Doris looked panic-stricken. Her hand flew up to her face to cover her nose. For a moment she looked up at Tad Baker, who was pretending to pay no attention to any of it. Then, she dove back into the pool.

Tad Baker blew his whistle at her. "No diving off the sides of the pool," he told her apologetically. Doris swam away frantically.

"Ha, you got rid of her," laughed Marsha.

"This feud never ends, does it?" Mike said, shaking his head and laughing.

"She's just too horrible for words," Marsha told him. She drew Mike away from the lifeguard stand. "Is Doris chasing Tad Baker these days?" she asked, eager for some juicy Doris gossip.

"I guess so," he answered. "She's always swimming under his stand and hanging around the office when he's there."

"Poor guy," Marsha sympathized.

"A lot of my friends would call him a lucky guy," Mike corrected her. "Doris isn't exactly homely, you know."

"Yuck, there's no accounting for taste," Marsha replied, scrunching up her nose in disgust. "Does Tad like her?"

"I don't know. I think he's interested. Tad's a real nice guy. He was in chemistry with me last year."

Lena and Sara joined them. "Did I say something wrong again?" Lena asked. "I just wanted her to know that her makeup was coming off."

"Don't worry about it," Sara assured her. "I'm going on the diving board."

"I too. I love to dive," Lena said, following her.

The line for the high diving board was fairly long. As she stood on it, Sara saw Doris huddling with her friends Craig and Heather. *I wonder what she's up to now,* Sara thought. She saw Craig shake his head, no. Then she saw Doris stamp her foot and pout. *Uh, oh,* Sara told herself, *when she does that pouting bit, Craig the spineless wonder does whatever she tells him to do.*

Sara's turn came for the board and she walked to the

edge and did a cannonball into the pool. She went straight to the bottom of the eleven-foot deep diving area. She loved the weightless, soundless sensation of swimming back to the top.

She broke the surface and swam over to the ladder. She was about to pull herself up when Lena walked out onto the board.

Lena did a bounce at the end of the board. As she did, Sara was aware of a mooing sound. She followed it and saw that Craig Lawrence had gotten hold of a lifeguard's bullhorn and was mooing into it. *Moooooooooooo,* he intoned deeply with every bounce Lena took on the board. Glancing at Lena, Sara realized it was true: Lena did look like a big pink cow bouncing on the diving board.

"Stop that," Sara shouted at Craig.

Mooooooooooooooo.

Sara looked up to see how Lena was dealing with this embarrassment. To her surprise and dismay, she saw Lena standing on the board smiling and waving. Sara pivoted around to see Heather and Doris snickering and waving back to Lena.

Sara noticed that the people all around the pool area were laughing and pointing at Lena. Suddenly Tad Baker blew his whistle and motioned for Lena to dive.

Lena's dive was perfect, but people were still laughing at the mooing.

"You must have been so mortified," Sara sympathized.

"They were just making a joke," Lena said. "At my uncle's home at the lake we sometimes bang a cowbell when someone jumps off the board."

"Why were you waving at them?" Sara asked.

"I thought it would be better if they did not think they were angering me. That was their intention, was it not?"

Marsha ran up to meet them. "That was awful!" she declared.

"I am used to this kind of joke," Lena told them, shrugging her shoulders, but not meeting their eyes. "I seem to attract people who like to play this sort of prank. I just try to pretend it does not bother me. That is what I always do."

Marsha gave Sara a look that said, "How terrible for her," and decided to drop the subject.

"Hey, look who's here," said Sara, looking up the ramp that led from the pool locker rooms to the main pool area.

Rissa was walking toward them. "It was too hot to stay home," was the way she explained her change of heart.

The girls spent another hour swimming. They saw Doris and Heather from time to time, but they managed to avoid them.

"Even with the lotion, I am burning," Lena said, examining her porcelain white arms, which were turning pink. "I am going to change."

"We'll be up in a few minutes," said Rissa. "Wait for us in the locker room."

When Marsha, Rissa, and Sara arrived in the locker room, they saw no sign of Lena. "Where could she have gone to?" Marsha wondered aloud for all of them.

Sara looked in the front, Marsha searched out by the pool, and Rissa checked the ladies' room. Still no Lena.

They met again in the locker room. "She couldn't possibly still be getting dressed, could she?" asked Rissa. At once they checked the feet in the stalls, but all the bare feet looked more or less alike.

Pssssst.

The three girls heard the sound at once. They spun around in three different directions trying to locate it.

"I am over here in this booth," came a low whisper that was unmistakably Lena's heavily accented voice. "Someone has taken all my clothes."

"What do you mean?" asked Marsha.

"I was taking off the wet bathing suit and I threw it on the door, so," her hand rapped the top of the stall door. "I bent over to dry myself, and when I reached for my clothes which I had also draped on the door—Ach!—nothing was there. No bathing suit, no clothing, nothing."

The three girls looked at each other. "Doris!" they said in unison.

"Now what are we going to do?" wailed Sara, who was getting worn out from one Lena-related mishap after another.

"She must have dumped the clothing somewhere," Marsha suggested. "Let's look." They searched in the ladies' bathroom, in the other open lockers, and under all the benches. Nothing.

"I give up," cried Sara, throwing her hands in the air. "I'm going to have to go all the way home and come all the way back with clothing. Meanwhile Lena is going to have to stand here shivering for over an hour."

"Hold on a minute," said Rissa. "Maybe we can figure something out. I have a dry tank suit in the lifeguards' office that you can borrow," she offered.

Rissa got the suit and Marsha donated her shorts since she was wearing a long T-shirt. But they were too small for Lena, so Rissa gave Lena hers and squirmed into Marsha's shorts.

By the time they were done, Lena had on Rissa's suit and shorts. Rissa wore her own bathing suit and Marsha's too-tight shorts. Marsha's long T-shirt was now a teeny-tiny mini-dress and she kept tugging the hem self-consciously.

"I hope we don't meet anyone we know on the way home," said Sara. "You guys look pretty weird."

"You're just lucky you're too skinny for us to borrow your clothes," Rissa growled. This day was not going well at all.

Feeling slightly ridiculous, the girls made their way out of the locker room. At the bottom of the stairs they saw Heather and Doris sitting on a bench fooling with a Polaroid camera.

"Where are Lena's clothes?" Marsha demanded.

Doris acted as if Marsha hadn't spoken. She turned to Heather. "Now there's a pretty funny shot," Doris said, indicating the four girls.

"I'll kill you, you twerp!" shouted Rissa, lunging for Doris. In the next second there was a loud RIIIIIP! and a pop as Rissa's tight shorts split down the back and the snap popped open.

The shorts began sliding down Rissa's hips. She grabbed at them as Doris leaped out of her reach. Marsha ran over to Doris, clutching the hem of her long T-shirt to her sides. "You give back those clothes!" she shouted.

"Smile," Doris taunted as Heather snapped a picture. Just then a car horn honked. Heather and Doris both ran quickly toward the deep green Jaguar that pulled close to the parking lot curb.

Rissa had slipped out of her shorts and was about to chase the girls, wearing only her tank suit. Marsha stopped her. "Leave them alone," she said. "We work here. If we get caught fighting with the people who come to the pool we'll lose our jobs. They're not worth it. Besides, I think that was Doris's mother in the car."

"We should tell her mother what Doris did," yelled Sara, coming up behind them.

"Doris would just deny it," Marsha replied.

Rissa's blue eyes blazed with anger. "It would feel so good just to connect with her snotty little face," Rissa snarled, wrapping her towel around her waist.

"I'd like to see that," agreed Sara. Marsha, Sara, and Rissa continued to grumble and let off steam, talking about what they'd do to Doris and Heather if they got their hands on them. Soon they had come up with tortures so ridiculously horrible that they had to laugh, despite their anger. They almost forgot about Lena who stood off quietly to the side, just watching.

Chapter Five

"Today will be better," Sara said as the three of them stepped off the bus. "It even started off better. We all have one o'clock shifts so we didn't have to get up early. We get a break from Lena, at least for a few hours while she's at her lit class, the sun is shining—"

"Oh, be quiet," said Rissa, who was still upset about blowing her audition.

"You don't have to be so crabby," Sara shot back. "We all have our problems. I have to work with Merry Meyer again today."

Marsha couldn't take any more of their bickering so she walked ahead toward the baby-sitting center. She scanned the park bulletin board for any interesting new announcements. A Polaroid picture caught her attention immediately. She walked up to the board and saw, to her horror, that the picture was the one Heather had taken the day before.

Up front was Rissa, looking demented with rage and grabbing at her falling shorts. Behind her stood Marsha with her mouth open, shouting and clutching her mini-T-shirt dress to her sides with clenched fists. Sara stood with her face screwed into an expression of outrage. Behind them all stood Lena, in clothing too small for her, looking confused and unhappy.

The photo was attached to a piece of loose-leaf paper on which was written the caption: "What fashionable park employees and their friend are wearing this summer."

Sara and Rissa came up behind Marsha. "What a witch," said Sara.

Rissa pulled the photo off the bulletin board, crumpled it, and shoved it into her pocket. "Every time that girl turns around I'm going to blow my whistle until I get her thrown out of the pool," she threatened.

When Marsha arrived at the baby-sitting center she saw that the Peterson twins were already there. "It was a dark day for us when Mrs. Peterson discovered the Hemway Park babysitting center," Marsha's usually patient boss, Patty, had said to her. Adam and David Peterson were adorable-looking little kids with curly brown hair and big brown eyes who always wore identical striped shirts, but they were both spoiled and totally out of control. They had wills of iron when it came to getting whatever they wanted.

"I'm going to ask you to play with them," Patty told Marsha. "If you can keep them out of my hair, the rest of us can deal with the others."

Marsha spent the next half hour trying to interest the two five-year-olds in songs and a game of CandyLand, but they were intent on running around the center pretending to be Spiderman and Superman.

Patty and the other assistants were getting the kids ready for a walk around the park. The assistants loaded the little ones into wagons while Patty lined up the children who were old enough to walk.

"Want to go for a nice walk?" Marsha asked the twins.

"No!" shouted Adam.

"I want you to come to my secret hideout," yelled

David, pulling Marsha over to a kid-sized cardboard house. "I'm Superman and I've captured you."

Patty shot Marsha a sympathetic look as she herded the children out the door. "We'll just be over by the tennis courts if you need anything," she said.

"Okay," Marsha called over her shoulder. Adam and David pulled on each other's hands, testing their superhero strength.

"In the house. You're my prisoner!" shouted Adam, prodding Marsha into the small house.

"My prisoner!" protested David, pushing his brother.

Marsha tried to distract the quarreling boys. "I'm going into the jail now." She got on her hands and knees, opened the little cardboard flap door, and squeezed through the doorway. She knelt on the cardboard floor of the house and peeked out the small window at the twins.

"Aha!" cried Adam triumphantly. "Now you will never escape!" With that he grabbed up the long jump rope that lay by the house and handed David one end. David seemed to understand what his brother had in mind. Immediately the two of them began running around the house in opposite directions, wrapping the little house up in rope. They met and tied the ends of their rope into a knot.

"Hey, what are you two superheroes doing?" Marsha called out of the little window.

"We're making sure you never escape," shouted Adam. At first Marsha thought this was cute, but then it dawned on her that they were doing a pretty good job of securing her in the house. She pushed on the little cardboard door and found that it only opened a crack.

"That was a fun game. Now let me out," she called through the window.

"Never!" yelled David. "We're going out to catch more bad guys."

"No!" shouted Marsha. "You stay right here and untie these ropes."

"Trying to trick me, eh!" replied David, standing back with his hands on his hips. "No bad guy can fool Superman!"

"I mean it, David Peterson," Marsha scolded through the little window. "Untie these ropes now."

"Come on Spiderman," David told his brother. "Let's go fight crime."

How am I ever going to explain this? Marsha thought, panic-stricken. She began thumping her fists on the cardboard. It gave a little at the seams but it was sturdier than she'd expected. "Let me out of here!" she cried.

"The prisoner is going wild. We'd better leave," she heard Adam say.

Just then she heard a voice call. "Hello, is anybody here?" Marsha peeked out the window and saw that it was Jim.

"Jim, over here," she called, feeling completely idiotic. "Don't let those two monsters get past you!"

"We caught a bad guy!" Adam told Jim.

"I've come to take the prisoner to my secret bad guy super jail," Jim told the boy. "Give the prisoner to me."

Adam saluted Jim and the two twins set to work untying the ropes from around the house. Thoroughly embarrassed, Marsha climbed out the little door.

"I came by to see how you were doing. I guess I saw," Jim said with a laugh.

"I don't know what I would have done if you hadn't come along," Marsha said, smoothing down her hair. "Those two are impossible."

In several more minutes, Patty and the others

returned from their walk. Patty approached Marsha with Mrs. Peterson by her side. "How were my two angels?" asked Mrs. Peterson, patting her sons on the head.

"They got a little carried away with their superhero fantasy," Marsha said, trying to control herself.

"Yes, they're so imaginative," Mrs. Peterson replied. "And so high-spirited."

"They sure are," Marsha agreed. *That's certainly one way of looking at it, anyway,* she thought.

Patty let Marsha go early since things were slow after that. She and Jim walked around the park talking about the week-long bike trip Jim planned to take with a group in August. "Too bad you have this job," he said. "You could have signed up for it."

Marsha couldn't see herself biking through New England for hundreds of miles. It was definitely not her idea of a good time, but she decided not to dampen his enthusiasm. "It sounds like you'll have a great time," she said.

They sat down to rest on a picnic bench near a wooded area. Jim put his arm around Marsha. "I'm looking forward to it, but I'll miss you."

She felt herself freeze up. It wasn't that she didn't like Jim, and he really was kind of cute, with his wavy dark hair and green eyes. And so what if he was short? He was still taller than Marsha by almost two inches. But why did he have to ruin a perfectly nice conversation by getting all romantic?

He stroked the braid at the back of her head, and she knew that any minute he would try to kiss her. "You really bailed me out today," she began talking nervously. "Imagine if I'd had to tell Mrs. Peterson that I'd lost her two angels."

Jim wasn't listening. He leaned in and brushed her lips with his. She tried to kiss him back—but she just couldn't. "We'd better head to the gate if we're going to get the five o'clock bus," she said.

"What's the matter?" Jim asked, looking hurt.

"Nothing. We just have to catch that bus is all."

"Marsha, is it that you don't like me? Ever since you asked me to the June dance, I sort of figured we were going together."

"I like you a lot," she answered honestly. "Come on. I really have to be on that bus."

Jim sighed. They took the bus home together, but Marsha could feel that things weren't right between them. There was nothing wrong with Jim. So what was the matter with her?

Sara's day was equally frustrating. When Nicky came by to see her he found her running frantically between the two booths, Michael and Gabriel.

"She did it to me again!" cried Sara as she madly made change and gave out parking stubs. "Every time we get busy she runs to the bathroom. How can I complain to Mr. Meyer about his own daughter?"

"Doesn't he see that she's always gone?" Nicky asked.

"Mr. Meyer sees what he wants to see, it seems to me."

Suddenly there was a surge of cars and no sign of Merry. "Can I help?" Nicky offered.

Sara quickly explained the procedure to Nicky. He caught on fast and took over Merry's booth. Things were going well until Sara caught sight of Mr. Meyer heading in their direction.

"Duck down," she called to Nicky. "Don't let him see you or I'm dog meat." Nicky crouched low in the booth. Luckily there were no cars at that moment.

Mr. Meyer stopped at Sara's booth and inspected her dispenser numbers and counted out her cash drawer.

"Exactly correct," he complimented. "I may have misjudged you, Miss Marshall. You've been doing a fine job. Perhaps I let your . . . ahem . . . style, cloud my judgement."

"Thank you, Mr. Meyer," Sara answered, trying to block his view of the toll booth behind her.

At that moment Merry returned from the ladies' room. Thinking she'd be able to duck into her booth without her father knowing she was ever gone, she crouched low and tried to slip in.

"*Aaaaaaaahhhhh!*" she screamed as she unexpectedly tumbled over the crouching Nicky. "Help, Daddy! Help!"

Mr. Meyer leaped across the lane with a burst of speed Sara wouldn't have dreamed he had in him. He grabbed Nicky by the collar and looked as if he were about to punch him.

"Please Mr. Meyer," Sara shouted. "He's my friend. He was just helping me while Merry went to the bathroom."

"You let this . . . this . . . hippie, or punk, or whatever you kids call yourselves these days . . . you let him stand in Gabriel and be responsible for Hemway's parking fees!"

"He's really very honest—"

"There can be no excuse for this. I'm sure you could have handled Gabriel for the brief time it takes Merry to go to the ladies' room."

Brief time! thought Sara. *She's gone for forty-five minutes at a shot.* Even so, Sara couldn't bring herself to place the blame on Merry. It wasn't her fault she was a nervous wreck. Look who she had for a father!

"You have one more chance," he warned. "If it wasn't for your accuracy with the cash, I'd fire you on the spot. You have been warned twice now."

Mr. Meyer stormed back into his little green and

white shingled office. "What a bloody—" Nicky started but a warning look from Sara stopped him. Merry was right there.

"Sorry," she said with a nervous giggle. "You know how Daddy is about rules."

"I know," Sara said. "Rules are rules."

Rissa was on the lookout for Doris all that day. She wanted to find some way to make the girl's life miserable. She spotted her at three o'clock, but her job at the kiddie pool kept her from doing anything.

At four, Sara, Nicky, and Lena showed up for a swim. Rissa had a fifteen-minute break and was sitting with them on the chairs around the pool area. She noticed Sparks, a big shaggy dog that belonged to Mr. Monahan, the lifeguards' supervisor, running around. *That's odd,* she thought. *Monahan always ties him up near the office.*

"What's that dog got on?" Sara wondered out loud. He seemed to be wearing clothing. Rissa called the dog, "Here, Sparks, here, boy." The friendly dog ran over to her immediately.

"Those are my clothes," gasped Lena. The dog was dressed in Lena's stolen shorts and shirt. Her bathing suit was wrapped around the dog's neck. The dog had a handwritten sign tacked onto the shirt. It said: "I'm Lena, a real dog."

Lena looked confused. "Why is this girl doing all these things to me? Have I offended her?"

"It's not you," Sara assured her. "She hates us, and since you hang around with us, she hates you too. Your comment about her zit didn't help either, I guess."

"Oh," Lena moaned, "me and my mouth again."

"Don't feel bad, Lena," said Rissa. "You could get on Doris's bad side without saying a word. She's always looking for someone to torment. It's her hobby."

Rissa spotted Doris near the pool talking to Tad Baker. Doris was dressed in a short pink sundress and white sandals.

"So when are you going to be off?" Rissa heard Doris ask Tad flirtatiously.

Rissa blew her whistle. "No street clothing in the pool area," she announced.

"Come on Rissa, don't be such a hardnose," Tad objected.

"Those are the rules. You'll have to leave," Rissa insisted, red-faced with anger.

"Get lost," Doris snapped.

Rissa blew her whistle again. "All footwear worn in the pool area must have a rubber sole."

"Technically she's right," Tad told Doris apologetically.

"Who cares what she says," Doris replied. "She's just a big power-crazed goon."

With one swift motion Rissa shot her foot out, hooked it around Doris's ankle and snapped it back. Doris went flying backward into the pool.

Doris floundered around in the water comically, her curled hair sticking to her head, her mascara running down her face.

In seconds, Mike and Mr. Monahan came running. "What happened here?" cried Mr. Monahan, helping Doris up over the side.

"She pushed me into the pool!" screamed Doris. "Fire her!"

"I didn't push her," Rissa said.

"Okay, you tripped me then. It's the same thing."

"I warned you that street clothing, including sandals with no rubber soles, were forbidden in the pool area.

50

Those shoes are slippery when wet. I'm sorry you slipped, but I warned you."

Mike looked at Rissa with suspicion. She stared straight ahead. Mr. Monahan looked to Tad Baker. "What happened here?" he asked Tad.

Tad just held up his hands in a "beats me" gesture. "I was watching the swimmers in the pool," he lied. "I have no idea." Behind Mr. Monahan's back Rissa caught Tad's eye and mouthed "Thank you."

Mr. Monahan looked undecided for a moment. Then he caught sight of Sparks running loose. He quickly told Doris that she shouldn't have been in the pool area without the proper attire and ran off to get his dog. Shooting Rissa a look of pure hatred, Doris stomped off looking like a half-drowned cat.

"You can't do stuff like that," Mike whispered to Rissa after they'd walked a few paces away from everyone. "It'll get you fired."

"I didn't do anything," Rissa insisted coolly.

"Rissa."

"Okay, well, she had it coming. She's been tormenting Lena."

"The Swiss girl who told me I looked like a red zebra!" Mike asked in a loud whisper. "I thought you didn't like her. I thought she ruined your audition."

"I know," Rissa admitted, "but she kind of grows on you." Actually Rissa hadn't thought about it until just that moment, but it was true—she was actually beginning to like Lena. "She means well. She's just so big and gawky. In a way she reminds me of myself before . . . before . . . you know."

"When you were still a moth?" Mike asked.

Rissa smiled at him. "I didn't know you were so poetic," she said, to cover her pleasure at his remark. "That's sort of what I mean. Before the Makeover

51

Club helped me, helped all three of us stop feeling like . . ."

"Moths?"

"Yeah." Rissa was struck with a sudden idea. "Do you think the Makeover Club could help Lena? I was looking at that picture Doris took of us, you know, the one I told you about. At first I didn't notice it because I was so mad, but Lena didn't come out that badly in the picture. She has a pretty face if you stop and look at her. She's really photogenic."

Mike looked over at the large clumsy girl with her unstyled wispy blond hair. She was slumped down in her chair looking dejected and miserable. "I don't know. None of you ever looked quite as hopeless as she does."

"You forget," said Rissa, thinking back to her own pre-Makeover Club days. She'd had a straight, boyish figure, a nothing haircut that she had cut in the barber shop with her father, and had looked more like a boy than a girl. "I was pretty hopeless myself."

"I always liked you," Mike said. "I never saw a girl who could play a better game of basketball."

"You didn't *like* me, like me though," Rissa reminded him.

"Not like I like you, *like* you, now," Mike teased, taking her hand. She gave it a squeeze and continued to smile at him. They would have both felt funny kissing in such a public place, but, for a moment, they kissed with their eyes.

"That settles it," said Rissa after a few moments. "I'm calling an emergency meeting of the Makeover Club for this Saturday. Project Lena is about to begin."

Chapter Six

That night Sara called Marsha to tell her about Project Lena. "And of course, Rissa was her usual overbearing self," Sara recounted. "She showed Lena the picture Doris took of us and said it was clear from the photo that with a little improvement Lena could look much better than she does. She didn't even ask Lena if she wanted to be improved. Rissa just took it for granted that Lena knew she looked like a clod."

"How did Lena react?"

"At first she just looked at Rissa as if she were talking Chinese. Then Rissa ran up to the locker room and came back with a picture of her father and brothers and her that she's had in her wallet for a couple of years. Lena was impressed by how awful Rissa looked then. She agreed to join the Makeover Club, for the summer anyway.

"On the way home she asked me if she really looked that awful. I didn't know what to say. I just said everyone could use some improvement. She's acted mopey all evening. She's been in the shower for a half hour now. I think Rissa sort of overwhelmed her."

"I miss our weekly meetings," Marsha admitted. "It'll be fun to get back into things. Besides, I've gained back five pounds. I can diet and exercise with Lena."

"While we're fixing her up, maybe she can clue me into her secret for great skin. You have to admit her skin is terrific," observed Sara, who fought a constant battle with pimples.

"Where are we having the meeting?"

"Your house."

"Is that right?"

"You don't mind, do you?"

"No, I guess not. It would have been nice to be asked though. When Rissa gets something in her head, she just sort of steamrolls everyone around her."

The next day the girls met in Marsha's bedroom. Marsha had dragged out all the beauty books they'd bought for the Makeover Club. She also pulled out all the makeup, rollers, hair accessories, makeup brushes, eyelash curler, and other stuff she'd acquired since transforming herself from brainy, twerpy Marsha Kranton to brainy, pretty Marsha Kranton. She never used much of it. She simply did her shoulder-length brown hair up in a French braid for everyday, and set it in electric rollers for special occasions. She wore mascara and some blush, but often she went without makeup. Getting rid of her glasses had been a plus. Now she was thinking of getting clear contact lenses instead of the green-tinted ones she had. She tried to convince herself that the green looked natural, but it didn't. She noticed people staring into her eyes trying to figure out if they were her natural color.

Marsha thought back to last June. She'd originally made herself over to attract Craig Lawrence, but when Craig canceled their date for the dance, she'd asked Jim instead. She knew Jim liked her a lot—and she liked him.

She didn't understand why she had such a problem kissing him. She worried that she had some deep psychological hang-up. *I finally get a boyfriend and I can't even bring myself to kiss him,* she thought, disgusted with herself, feeling that the problem lay in some terrible weirdness inside her.

The doorbell rang and Marsha heard Sara saying hi to her parents, and the sound of Lena's accent. They soon tromped up the stairs.

Lena looked as if she were preparing to undergo surgery. She was very tense and serious.

"Don't worry," Marsha assured her. "We're all going to do it with you."

Rissa clomped up the stairs behind them. She carried a large blue tote that was crammed full of books and magazines. "Okay, let's get to it," she announced. "First of all, Lena, I'm going to have to be honest with you if we're going to get anywhere. Can you take it?"

"I believe so," Lena said, sounding uncertain.

"Okay, then, you have got to get some kind of weight loss and exercise program going. You're not really as fat as you look. I'd say you've got to lose about fifteen pounds and then tone up what you've got."

Rissa reached into her tote and pulled out a xeroxed piece of paper. "I found this diet in a magazine. It's nutritionally balanced, but you have to drink eight glasses of water each day along with eating these diet meals."

Marsha looked at the menus on the paper. "Boiled kale and carrot casserole, disgusting," she commented.

"I've signed us all up for Jazzercise class at the park," Rissa continued, "and Lena, I noticed you like to swim, so I signed you up for eight o'clock lap swim at the pool."

"But I have ten o'clock classes at the college," Lena protested.

"You can do both. You'll just have to get up bright and early," Rissa insisted.

Lena looked to Sara and Marsha for help. "No pain, no gain," they said in unison, voicing the phrase Rissa had repeated over and over to them last year.

"I'm glad I don't have to do all this stuff," said Sara, holding up her thin arms.

"You don't have to diet," Rissa said, "but you sure are going to Jazzercise with us. Look at you. No muscle tone at all."

"Okay, okay," Sara said, drawing her bony elbows into her sides.

"We could all use this," Marsha agreed. "We've all gotten sloppy."

"Well, not all of us," Rissa disagreed.

"Yes—*all* of us," Marsha said, and gave Rissa a slap on the behind.

Lena forced down her second glass of water of the day. Drinking eight glasses of water didn't sound difficult, but it was. By the end of the day Lena was sick of water, and she was tired of running to the bathroom every two minutes, as well. And, while the meals on their diet were healthy enough, Lena felt hungry all the time.

This trip to America was certainly turning out to be more than Lena had bargained for. She felt so lonely and homesick. She knew everything she was saying was going over badly, but she didn't know how to improve on it. Sara was right, she was trying too hard—trying to be too helpful, laughing too loud, wanting too much for everyone to like her. She knew it, but she couldn't stop doing it.

And then strange, bossy, Rissa had struck right to the heart of things. Lena always felt she had to try doubly hard to be liked because all her life she'd been a big, graceless girl. Never pretty. Never delicate like her younger sister, Frieda. Without ever admitting it to herself, Lena assumed that if she didn't try very hard to be helpful, accommodating, and pleasant, no one would bother with her.

But sometimes she picked the wrong words, especially when she had to speak English. It was so frustrating to constantly be saying the wrong thing, when the right thing was what she so desperately longed to say.

Maybe this plan would work. Perhaps if she looked better then she wouldn't have to try so hard to feel accepted. She could, as Sara suggested, finally *relax*.

Lena walked into the downstairs bathroom and studied herself in the mirror. She pulled her hair away from her wide, square face. "Big ears," she said disgustedly. Her blue eyes filled with tears. Who were they fooling? She would always be big, ugly Lena, trying too hard and being the brunt of jokes for the Dorises of the world.

"Come on, we're going to be late for Jazzercise," said Sara, knocking on the bathroom door.

Lena splashed water on her face and opened the door. Sara stood there with a big milk mustache on her face and an apple Danish in her hand.

"Time to Jazzercise," she said brightly. "Hurry up, Mike's going to drive us all there."

"Here we go," Lena agreed glumly.

The Jazzercise class was filled with women in brightly colored exercise outfits. Some of them stretched and warmed up for the class. Others stood in little groups and talked.

Rissa, Lena, Marsha, and Sara stood off by themselves in a corner. Marsha wore a black leotard and tights, Rissa wore a red jogging outfit, and Sara had on a bright pink-and-purple striped exercise outfit. Lena simply wore baggy shorts, a T-shirt, and beat-up white sneakers.

"My stomach is growling already," Marsha complained. "I need a roll or something for breakfast. I still feel hungry on that stupid diet. And I can hear the water sloshing around in my stomach whenever I walk."

"You cannot hear the water, Marsha," Rissa snapped. "That's all in your imagination, so stop complaining. The idea of the Makeover Club is to support one another not depress each other, remember."

"Don't you talk," Marsha shot back. "Nobody gets crabbier than you do when you're hungry, and I can tell from your tone of voice that you're hungry right now."

"Now, girls, please—" Sara began.

"Be quiet," Rissa and Marsha shushed her at once. The diet was putting them both in a bad mood.

Just then the Jazzercise instructor bounced into the room. She popped a cassette into the tape deck and called, "Spread yourselves out, standing."

The music was a bluesy ballad and she took them through a series of slow rolls and stretches to its tune. Marsha was dismayed to find that she could no longer get the palms of her hands to the floor as she could in the spring. It didn't comfort her much to see that Lena couldn't even reach the floor. In fact, Lena was already red in the face—and this was the warm-up!

The tape switched to a faster song by Michael Jackson. "Okay, now!" the instructor yelled, clapping her hands. "Three steps forward and clap . . . now three hops back and clap . . . and the same thing to the right . . . and now to the left."

A bit confused, the girls managed to keep up with

the pace. It seemed that everyone but them had this routine memorized.

"Now turn around, step right and kick left," the instructor shouted, demonstrating the step. Lena turned around, stepped left, and kicked right.

"Ouch!" yelled Marsha, who took the kick right in the shins.

"I am so sorry," Lena apologized. She stopped to look at Marsha's shin and collided with Rissa who was still following the instructor's routine. The collision propelled Lena back into Marsha, who reached out frantically for something to break her fall. What she found was Sara, whom she pulled down with her. The woman next to Sara was turning and kicking and tripped over Marsha and Sara who lay sprawled under her feet.

The instructor stopped. "Is everyone all right?" she asked.

"Fine," Marsha replied, kneeling, "except that I lost my contact lens."

Without another word everyone began crawling around on the ground looking for the lens as Michael Jackson sang away in the background.

"It's tinted green," Marsha told the Jazzercise class.

"Is this it?" Lena asked, peeling the small, mangled, green-tinted lens off the bottom of her sneaker.

"It sure is," Marsha observed. "It *was,* at any rate."

"Let's get back to it," the instructor called. "I want you to spin three times to the left and jump. Ready? Go!"

"Oww!" yelled Marsha, as Lena came spinning into her. "She said *left,* Lena!" Marsha had a feeling this was going to be a long class.

* * *

Project Lena was not easy. Lena never mastered keeping her left and right straight. Jazzercise was always a dangerous undertaking, but the girls soon became adept at staying clear of Lena's misdirected maneuvers.

They adapted their diet to add one snack a day. The snack brought their total caloric intake up from one thousand to thirteen hundred calories a day.

This change was agreed upon one afternoon after Rissa and Marsha almost strangled one another in a fight over who had the more disagreeable personality. Sara pointed out that they had both become very disagreeable since starting the diet. And, she added, Lena seemed dazed and subdued, like a person who was starving to death. Once they modified their diet, things went more smoothly.

Rissa swam with Lena every morning. Lena proved to be a strong swimmer with tremendous endurance. Even athletic Rissa sometimes tired before Lena.

By the last week in July, Project Lena had been going on for three weeks. The change in Lena was beginning to become evident. She'd lost twelve pounds and had toned up quite a bit.

"You're going to have to take in your clothes," Sara commented during a Saturday Makeover Club meeting at her house. "They're looking awfully baggy."

Sara was really wishing she could burn Lena's drab, unstylish clothing, but she knew Lena didn't have the money to simply go out and buy a whole new wardrobe.

"You're definitely going to need a new bathing suit," Rissa pointed out. "And you're going to need it two weeks from now."

"Why two weeks?" Marsha asked.

"Because two weeks from this Saturday Hemway is having a big Teen Luau night around the pool. There'll

60

be Hawaiian food and music, and swimming. Everyone is supposed to come wearing Hawaiian shirts and grass skirts and stuff over their bathing suits. That's when Lena is going to make her debut."

"What do you mean?" Lena asked, looking alarmed.

"I've been thinking about this a lot," Rissa explained. "No one has really noticed how you're changing because you still have the same big clothes and your hair and all is still the same. Since Doris hasn't been around for the last two weeks—Tad Baker told me she was away with her family and would be gone for another week and a half—she won't know what hit her when you show up at the Luau looking gorgeous. Just let her try to make fun of you then."

"How do we know she'll be at the Luau?" Sara asked.

"Because all the lifeguards and juniors have to work the Luau. If Tad is there, Doris will be there."

"I do not know," said Lena. "It seems so close, this Luau. I am not even sure why I am doing this."

"Lena!" cried Rissa, exasperated. "Aren't you angry about all the mean things Doris has done to you? Wouldn't you like to see her shocked expression when you show up looking gorgeous?"

"You really think this would make her like me?" Lena asked.

"You're missing the point!" Sara shouted. "You don't want her to like you. You want her to leave you alone. If you don't look like such an obvious . . . target, then she will."

"I suppose," Lena said, unconvinced.

"That's not the point, Sara," Marsha argued. "The point is that if Lena looks good, she'll feel better about herself. I've lost seven pounds on this diet, and that makes me feel good."

The girls continued to debate what the real purpose of Project Lena was, completely forgetting about Lena herself. Lena sat on Sara's bed and studied her face in the mirror across the way. She saw that cheekbones were beginning to emerge on her previously pudgy face. The thinning of her face made her eyes look larger and all the exercise seemed to have made them brighter. Still, she couldn't quite believe that these outward changes would have the effect her new friends thought they would. Wouldn't she still be big, tactless Lena on the inside?

"This is the agenda for the next two weeks," Rissa announced. "Exercise and swimming continue. Next Saturday we work on makeup and jazzing up your clothes with belts and scarves and stuff. During the week we go get you a new bathing suit. Then next Saturday, before the Luau, we'll get you a good haircut. Do you have enough money to afford that stuff?"

"I think so."

"Good, then we're all set."

Chapter Seven

The next two weeks were extremely busy ones. Lena's exercise and diet program knocked another five pounds off her weight and revealed a strong, curvaceous figure that no one would have guessed she possessed.

The girls let the lady at the makeup counter at Salzman's Pharmacy do Lena's face. "You have such beautiful skin," the woman complimented Lena honestly. "I'm going to try a bit of dusty pink blush right on your cheekbones here."

The makeup saleswoman used a broad brush to stroke Lena's cheekbones. "I'm going to give you a very natural look," she told Lena. She brushed a cream-colored eyeshadow under Lena's brow to her eyelids. She filled in the crease of Lena's eye with a darker brown shadow and then smudged the two colors together. She coated Lena's blonde lashes with a brown mascara and then lightly tinted Lena's blonde eyebrows with a touch of the mascara. "Eyebrow pencil is just too harsh a look for a girl as fair as you are," she explained, blending the mascara into Lena's brows.

Marsha was surprised to see how long Lena's lashes looked after the woman applied mascara. "Blondes often have blonde-tipped lashes so you can't see their real length," the woman said, stepping back to admire her handiwork. "A touch of dusty pink lipstick, and I'd say you were finished."

"You look great," Rissa said truthfully. Sara and Marsha nodded. They were just a little shocked at how pretty Lena really did look.

One evening the girls took the bus to the mall and selected a red two-piece bathing suit for Lena. "I cannot wear this," Lena protested in the fitting room.

"You can to," Sara assured her. "You look extremely sexy in it."

Lena sighed and did a few turns in front of the mirror. Sexy? Lena couldn't even begin to think of herself like that. "I just feel naked," she said. "I cannot feel comfortable in this."

In the end, they settled on a one-piece electric blue suit cut high on the sides and low in the back. "It goes great with your eyes," Marsha commented.

"Who would have ever dreamed you were built like Christie Brinkley," Sara said.

"Is that good or bad?" Lena asked.

"That's totally excellent," Sara assured her.

All that remained was for Lena to get her hair cut. The Saturday morning before the Luau, the three girls escorted her down to the unisex cutters on Hillside Avenue. They sat on the couch in the waiting area and paged through the magazines. After much debate, they decided on a short curly-top cut.

When they showed the picture to the stylist she frowned. "Her hair won't take that kind of curl, even with a perm," she said. "Let me try a cut I think would work."

The girls agreed and the stylist went to work. Thirty minutes later Lena had a cut that caused her straight hair to curve slightly just under her chin and long blunt bangs that skimmed her eyebrows. "Use a brush to blow it out very straight and then tuck it under," the stylist instructed Lena. "I used some mousse to give it extra body. Do you like it?"

Lena nodded and smiled.

"Five hours until countdown," Rissa said. "I can't wait until Doris sees the new you!"

Lena eyed herself in the mirror nervously but she smiled even wider.

At five o'clock that night Sara was busy blow-drying a green cellophane hula skirt she'd found in the costume box in the attic. The skirt and four plastic leis were coated with dust so Sara had given them a shower and was now speeding the drying time.

She was heading downstairs to get the iron to flatten the crinkled cellophane strips of the skirt when she passed by Lena sitting on the edge of the bed wearing her new bathing suit.

"What are you doing? You're supposed to be getting ready," Sara scolded.

"I cannot do this. I do not know where to begin," Lena whispered.

"I'll help you," Sara offered. She took a large, red-fringed cotton scarf and tied it around Lena's waist so that it draped over one leg and left the other exposed. She ran back to her room and returned with two of the damp leis. She shook them out and put them over Lena's head.

Sara squinted and examined Lena critically. She ran back into her room and returned with a handful of jewelry. "Since this is your big night, I'll lend you my favorite jewelry. My father bought me these in China-town and I keep them for special occasions. And tonight is special," she said.

She slid three carved ivory bangles onto Lena's arms. Then she went to put the large matching ivory loop earrings on Lena but quickly remembered that

Lena didn't have pierced ears. Inspired, she slid the loops off the gold hooks and held them in place with the catch from a small set of Elaine's clip-on earrings.

"I don't even want to be seen next to you, you look so great," Sara joked. Lena did look beautiful. She stared at herself in the mirror, her expression one of disbelief.

"It is as if I have become someone else," she said dreamily. "But I do not know who."

"Wow, this place looks so different," said Marsha to Sara and Lena. They were standing on the ramp leading down to the pool. Below them the pool area was lit with colored lanterns strung all around. The pool was lit from below making the water appear to shimmer. Plastic palm trees lined the pool edges. Hawaiian music wafted through the warm night air from the pool speaker system.

Marsha waved to Rissa, Mike, and Roger who stood behind the refreshment table. All the workers wore leis over blue T-shirts that said "Hemway Luau" on them.

Rissa waved back. When she caught sight of Lena she grinned to indicate her approval.

As they had planned, they met Jim and Nicky at the entrance.

"Kawabunga!" Nicky greeted them. Next to him was Jim, wearing a Hawaiian shirt and yellow clamdigger pants.

Nicky wore a thick grass skirt, sandals, about ten leis instead of a shirt, and brightly colored cardboard bracelets on his upper arms.

"Me Big Kahuna of all Hawaiian islands," Nicky joked in a deep voice. "You be Queen Kahuna," he said, grabbing Sara to his side tightly.

"You look nice," Jim complimented Marsha, who was wearing a long, loose shift with palm trees printed

66

on it. Her brown hair was loose and wavy from her braids. She'd caught it up on one side and stuck a silk orchid into the barrette.

"Thanks, so do you," she answered. She smiled at him brightly. She knew things had been strained between them, but she wanted to make this night fun.

"And who is this stranger?" asked Nicky gallantly of Lena.

Lena smiled at him shyly.

"You haven't been merely made over," he continued, "you have been transformed, elevated, exalted, intensified—"

"All right, that's enough," said Sara, fighting down a twinge of jealousy. Jealous of Lena? That was crazy.

The pool area was starting to fill up with teens. Marsha saw a few of the assistants from the baby-sitting center. Sara caught sight of Merry Meyer sitting next to a handsome boy. Sara and Marsha nudged each other when they both caught sight of Doris at the same time. As usual, she was surrounded by her group of adoring fans.

Doris looked great, as always. She had on a gold lamé hula skirt that sparkled under the colored lanterns. Her leis looked like they were made of real flowers and they draped gracefully over the curves of her revealing bathing suit top. Her hair was set in abundant curls held back with a network of gold lamé cords.

As Lena walked with her friends down toward the pool area, she sensed that all eyes were on her. She saw boys turn around from their conversations and stare at her. Even girls stopped to look at this statuesque blonde who looked as if she'd stepped out of a fashion magazine. Lena was causing a stir.

Over at the refreshment table Roger couldn't stop raving about Lena. "I'm in love," he moaned, clutching his heart and fluttering his eyes comically. "Love, I tell you, love."

"Look!" Rissa said with a laugh, "Doris just caught sight of Lena. Look at her face. She's totally confused."

Doris and Heather were in a huddle. Every few moments they'd stop whispering to look at Lena. Marsha could just imagine what the conversation sounded like. "Is that her?" "Couldn't be." "Is it?"

The Hawaiian music snapped off. After a crackle of static, rock music boomed out of the intercom.

"Care to dance?" came a voice from behind Lena.

Sara pinched Marsha. It was Tad Baker. This was too, too good to be true. Lena just stared off into space. Sara kicked her in the foot.

"What? What?" Lena sputtered.

"He asked if you wanted to dance," Sara told her as Tad smiled and waited.

"Me? I didn't know you were talking to me," Lena apologized. "Yes, I would like very much to dance."

Lena was a surprisingly good dancer. She and Tad looked like they were made for each other, both of them tall, blond, and gorgeous.

"Doris is turning purple," Rissa told Mike gleefully as they dished sweet and sour pork with pineapple bits onto paper plates and set them out. "Tad Baker. It couldn't be better."

After the dance Tad had to go back to his station at the soda stand, but different boys asked Lena to dance for just about every dance.

"The Makeover Club really outdid itself this time," Mike told Rissa.

"What do you mean *outdid* itself?" Rissa asked. "If you think she's so gorgeous, you go dance with her."

"I just meant that she needed much more work than

68

any of you did," Mike said calmly. "You wanted her to look good, didn't you?"

"I know, I just . . ."

"You're just jealous. I like it."

Tad Baker asked Lena to dance every time he was free. Rissa, Marsha, and Sara kept looking over to see how Doris was reacting. It was clear that she was beside herself.

Sara couldn't resist the urge to taunt Doris. She sauntered over to her. "Don't they make a lovely couple?" Sara said, nodding toward Lena and Tad.

Doris ignored Sara. Instead she grabbed Craig by the wrist and led him over to the dance area. "Come on, Craigy," she ordered. "Let's show them how to dance." Craig was delighted at this sudden interest from Doris. He walked eagerly toward the dance area.

Doris threw her head in a circle and danced frenetically. Craig, more wooden, tried to keep up. Doris twirled around and swiveled her hips. She was so good that a crowd gathered around to watch her and Craig. Doris's skirt spun out around her. Hundreds of dazzling, light-catching strands swirled past her shapely legs. The crowd was clapping and hooting enthusiastically.

When the music stopped, Doris smiled, breathless but wearing a triumphant expression. She looked around, searching the crowd for Tad. When the crowd parted she saw him.

He was holding Lena in his arms. The two of them were dancing together slowly, even though the music had stopped.

Chapter Eight

The days after the Luau were the most overwhelming ones Lena had ever experienced. Her classes at the college were over and she spent all her time down at the Hemway Park pool. Lena had never realized that there were so many boys her age at the pool. They seemed to be coming out of nowhere. When she went to the soda machine, a boy offered to open the flip top of her soda. When she sat and sunned herself another boy offered to share his lotion. Some of the boys who approached her were sweet; other boys were too forward and they made her nervous.

Lena noticed another remarkable change in her life. She didn't seem to be saying as many tactless things. She didn't need to try so hard to be accepted. She was relaxing. And even when she did stick her foot in her mouth, people seemed to respond better. They took her blunders as sarcastic remarks. She couldn't help but feel that was a bit unfair. *But why look the gift horse in the mouth?* she asked herself philosophically.

Tad Baker was by her side whenever possible. He asked her to the movies but she told him honestly that she was forbidden to date until she was seventeen.

"What about lunch?" he asked her, his blue eyes bright with infatuation. "I could come by for you in the day tomorrow. That's not a date. It's just . . . lunch.''

Lena agreed, feeling slightly guilty about fudging her mother's dating rules, but convincing herself it was just . . . lunch, after all. The truth was that of all the boys who were suddenly paying attention to her, Tad Baker was the one she liked best. *So handsome, so sweet,* she sighed to herself.

One day while Lena was sitting on a deck chair, talking nose to nose with Tad before his shift, Rissa came bounding up to them. ''Seen Mike?'' she asked, her face lit up with a smile.

''Behind the pump house,'' Tad told her. ''You look like you just won the lottery.''

''I did. I practically did. I got the job on the commercial! Remember, Lena? The commercial you, Sara, and Marsha almost wrecked for me. Well, it doesn't matter, because I got it! Roger just called me from home and told me they said I was exactly the type they were looking for and they thought I showed great poise considering what happened. Can you believe it? They want me to report next week.''

Mike came up behind her just in time to hear the last of her sentence. ''Report where?''

''To the city for my commercial. I'm going to be on TV!''

''That's great,'' Mike said flatly. ''Congratulations.''

''You don't sound very sincere,'' Rissa challenged him.

''I said congratulations, didn't I?''

''I'm going to need some time off, okay, Mike?'' Rissa said sweetly, not wanting to spoil her happiness with a fight.

''When?''

71

"We shoot the commercial all next week."

"No way, I'm sorry," he said. "I have one guy out sick. And Terry asked for time off a month ago. I'm too short staffed."

"Do you want me to pass up this job?"

"You should have thought of that before you took *this* job," he snapped at her.

Rissa felt tears and anger rising in her at the same time. How could he be so mean? Why was he acting this way?

"Just a moment," Lena spoke up. "I have my Senior Lifesaving Certificate from the Red Cross. I could take your job for the week, while you are in the city being in your commercial."

"You have your *Senior* Lifesaving?" Rissa asked.

"Fine," said Mike, still sounding angry. "I'll check with Monahan and test you tomorrow. If everything's okay, then you're hired." Mike turned to Rissa, "Then I'll see about getting you your job back if you should decide you want it back." With that he turned and walked away.

Rissa chased him and grabbed him by the back of his white polo shirt. "What do you mean getting my job back?"

"I can't hold a spot open for you to come and go as you please," he shouted. "Just because we go out together, do you think you're entitled to special treatment?"

"That's not fair! I do a good job and I've never asked for a thing!" she shouted back at him.

"What do you call this?"

"I call this meanness. Plain old, rotten, jealous meanness!"

She didn't want him to see her cry so she ran up the ramp and into the ladies' locker room. She found a booth in the bathroom, slammed the door shut, and leaned her forehead into the wall. Tears welled up in her eyes. If she loved Mike, how could she possibly hate him as much as she did right now?

Rissa got home from Hemway Park at about five. She wanted nothing more than to go to her room and be left alone but when she walked into the house she stopped, awestruck at what she saw. The house was neat. There was no baseball equipment on the stairs, no jackets piled at the end of the bannister, no skateboards lined up in the hallway. Rissa heard the sound of laughter coming from the kitchen.

Roger stuck his head out of the kitchen. Rissa waved for him to come closer. "What happened here?" she whispered.

Roger smiled. "Pete came home like a madman earlier today. He made everyone help him clean the place up. Don't open any of the closets too quickly or an avalanche of junk may come crashing down on your head."

"What's going on?"

"His girlfriend is here. She's cooking dinner for him—for all of us."

Rissa suddenly felt sick. She had so much to think about and this was just one more complicating thing.

Rissa followed Roger into the kitchen. Her brother Fred and the twins sat around the table smiling. Her father sat with them, his eyes practically twinkling with happiness.

At the stove stood a small dark-haired woman with large brown eyes. She wore a blue blouse with ruffles and a dark blue straight skirt under a flowered apron. She was stirring a large pot of something that smelled of tomatoes.

"Mary, this is my daughter Clarissa." Her father

73

introduced them. "Clarissa, Mary Giffone. She's the woman you've been so curious to meet."

Rissa shook the woman's extended hand. *She's got little bird bones,* Rissa thought. *I could break her hand if I squeezed too hard.*

"Hello, Clarissa," the woman greeted her. "I've been promising your father I'd cook him my famous chicken cacciatore for some time, so he suggested I come over and make some for all of you. I've heard so much about you, Clarissa. Your father brags about you all the time."

You don't have to butter me up, Rissa thought sourly. "Thanks, and please call me Rissa," she said. "Nobody in this family does, but since you're not in this family, I wish you would."

"All right, Rissa," Mary agreed, looking suddenly ill at ease.

Rissa wondered why she felt as if she'd insulted the woman. She'd simply spoken the truth. Mary wasn't a member of their family.

As the evening went on Rissa decided that she didn't like Mary one bit. She was icky sweet with the boys, laughing at all their dumb jokes and looking so gaga interested in every boring thing they had to say. And when Pete spoke, forget it. You'd have thought the wisdom of the ages was being poured at her feet.

The dinner was delicious, but that brought up another thing that was annoying Rissa—this woman was the most feminine woman on earth. She walked right in and immediately started cooking. And when dinner was over she looked to Rissa to help her clear the table. "I'm sorry," Rissa objected, as politely as she could manage. "It's Fred's turn tonight."

"I guess I'm not very liberated," Mary said with a laugh.

"I guess not!" Rissa replied tartly.

74

"Clarissa Jean," her father warned. How dare he scold her in front of this stranger. This was too much!

"I have a headache. I'd like to go to bed," she said stiffly.

"Clarissa," her father warned again.

"Try putting a warm cloth on your head," the woman cut in. "That always works for me. Good night. I hope you feel better."

Rissa wished Mary good night and went to her room as quickly as possible. The nerve of that woman to just march into her house and change the rules. And to insinuate that she was some kind of serving class of person just because she was female! No way.

And her father! What a betrayal. After a lifetime of making her feel that there was something wrong with her for being a girl, he went and picked the most frilly froo-froo woman he could find. It wasn't fair.

Rissa lay on her bed and cried. The people around her seemed so untrue: her father, Mary Giffone, Mike—and even Lena. It suddenly hit Rissa that she was furious at Lena for scooping her job out from under her. Who did Lena think she was, offering to just step in and take Rissa's spot, as if just anyone could do the job as well as Rissa did it. And after everything she'd done for Lena!

Rissa buried her face in her pillow and let her tears flow. Why were people so horrible? Why was life so confusing?

Chapter Nine

Marsha stood in the aisle of the Rosemont library and stared at the titles in the psychology section: *Normal Adolescence, The Art of Growing,* rows of books by Sigmund Freud and Carl Jung. She didn't know where to begin.

Marsha had come to the library hoping to figure out what was wrong with her. It had happened again at the Luau, and then again at the movies. She just didn't want to nuzzle with Jim the way he wanted to. It wasn't like he was overstepping the bounds, either. He just wanted to hold her hand, give her a kiss and a hug.

Marsha really liked Jim too. She wasn't interested in anyone else. She'd completely gotten over her infatuation with Craig Lawrence. In fact, Craig seemed sort of moronic to her now. *Strange,* she thought, *how a person's feelings can change so much from one month to the next.*

She pulled a book from the shelf and tried to read it. It was full of words like id, superego, displacement, transference. *Forget it,* thought Marsha. They may call me The Brain, but I'm not ready for this.

She walked over to the magazine section and plopped onto one of the low, tweedy couches. Maybe it was Jim's fault. He was nice, but he never did anything particularly romantic. She'd even had to invite him to the June dance. The truth of it was, he just wasn't thrilling, at least not to her. He would have been fine as a brother, or a friend—but not as a boyfriend.

She couldn't tell him that, though. It would hurt his feelings too badly. She just couldn't do that to him.

Marsha looked at the clock. It was almost four. Marsha left the library and wandered out to the bus stop. *Too hot to walk,* she thought. *Might as well take the bus home.*

When the bus pulled up, Marsha climbed on and was immediately greeted by a familiar voice. "Marsha! We are back here." It was Lena—and she was sitting with Jim. They were smiling and looked as if they had been having a lively conversation.

She walked to the back of the bus and took an available seat in front of them. "Hi," said Jim. "Lena and I were at Hemway. Were you at the library?"

"Uh-huh," Marsha said, feeling guilty about her reason for being there.

"How come?" he asked.

"Just looking for something to read," she lied.

"I want to talk to you about Rissa," Lena said, turning suddenly serious.

Marsha didn't want to have this conversation. Rissa had been busy shooting her commercial in the city for the last two days and Lena had been taking her place at the pool. Marsha thought Rissa should have been grateful to Lena for taking her place, but Rissa insisted on making cracks about Lena. She clearly didn't like the idea that Lena had taken her place.

"I do not understand what I did wrong. Why is Rissa angry with me?" Lena asked. "Sara says not to worry about it, but I cannot help worrying. Rissa has been a good friend to me."

"Sometimes Rissa likes to be number one at everything," Marsha tried to explain. "She's very competitive. It doesn't make sense, I know."

The situation was obviously upsetting Lena. Jim told her a few jokes to try to cheer her up. Marsha thought the jokes were dumb, but Lena laughed at them with her loud snorting laugh. Marsha was surprised to see how well Lena and Jim got along. They were laughing and giggling the whole way home.

The bus let them off at the corner of Hillside and Willis Avenues. Jim and Marsha had to go in one direction. Lena waved as she went off in the opposite direction.

"We sure misjudged that Lena," Jim said. "She really is a lot of fun. Such a great sense of humor. And her laugh is kind of nice in a goofy way, once you get used to it."

"You like that laugh?" Marsha asked, unbelieving.

"It's strange, but I like it. The other thing about Lena is that she has so much energy. She really goes for things. What a change in her. Who would have guessed that she'd turn out to be really fine looking."

Marsha just looked at him. Where was this sudden interest in Lena coming from? *Gee,* she thought, *laugh at this guy's jokes and he's all yours.*

"Lena seems to really hear you when you talk too," he continued. "She makes you feel like what you have to say is funny and important."

"Don't I make you feel that way?" Marsha asked.

"Not always. A lot of the time it seems like you're a million miles away."

"I'm sorry," she said sincerely. She hadn't realized it showed.

"I guess that's just how you are," he said glumly.

Marsha looked at him and it occurred to her that he

was getting fed up with her lukewarm attitude. Lena had made him feel good about himself.

She was suddenly afraid he would break up with her. She didn't want to be thrown over—and especially not for Lena. Lena was much too tall for him, but you never knew. She was laughing pretty hard at his jokes.

"I'm not like that, really I'm not," she said, taking his arm. "I've just had a lot on my mind lately. You know I really like you, Jim. I'm sorry I've been such a dud. I like you a lot."

He stopped and looked at her. "Do you? I've been doubting it. It seems to me that this just isn't working out. You just don't seem that interested, Marsha."

"I am interested," she said, clutching his arm. As she said it, it seemed absolutely true. She did like him and she didn't want to be without a boyfriend.

She grabbed him and kissed him hard on the lips. At first he was startled, but then he held her tightly and kissed her back equally hard. It seemed to her that they kissed for a long time. Her head was spinning. Part of her wanted to run away and another part wanted to stay with him, kissing, forever.

When the kiss finally ended they walked on home together hand in hand. They hardly spoke, but she could see that Jim was happy. She knew he was hers again, and that made her happy too.

You're not taking my boyfriend, Lena, she said to herself.

When Lena arrived home Sara was busy sewing up in her room. "What are you doing?" Lena asked, popping her head into the room.

Sara was startled and looked up guiltily. She hid what she was working on behind her. "Nothing. I mean, the strap of my bra broke and I'm sewing it."

Lena looked perplexed. "I didn't think you wore a—"

"Well, I do," Sara snapped, "sometimes. You're not the only one around here with curves, you know."

"I did not mean to offend . . . ach, me and my mouth," Lena said. "I will still go to band practice with you, ya?"

Sara had forgotten she'd promised to take Lena to rehearsal with her. She wasn't exactly in the mood for Lena today, but she had promised. "Okay, sure."

When Lena left, Sara took her sewing project from behind her back and looked at it dejectedly. *I never could sew,* she reminded herself. She'd been trying to sew socks into one of Elaine's bras to give herself a bustier figure.

She got up and tried on the stuffed bra. It flapped loosely around her ribcage. One sock came miserably unraveled and tumbled under the elastic at the bottom of the bra.

The reason for this sudden interest in cleavage was a conversation she'd overheard Nicky and Jim having about Lena. She was at the pool one day and had decided to sneak up behind the boys, who were sitting together, in order to startle them.

Before they knew she was near, she overheard Jim say, "That Lena is really stacked, isn't she?"

"She sure looks good in that bathing suit," Nicky had agreed.

Sara looked up to see that they were watching Lena taking a bounce before she dove off the board. They were focusing on a particular part of Lena's anatomy that was bouncing more than the rest of her.

Sara looked down at her own flat chest. *I'm not completely flat,* she told herself hopefully, even if she didn't need to wear a bra.

After that day she'd wondered if Nicky would like

80

her more if she were chestier. Maybe that was the reason he never wanted to make their relationship official. Perhaps he was waiting for a more "womanly" girl to come along.

Sara wasn't going to give up that easily. She'd looked at padded bras in the store, but they just didn't give her enough. That thin little layer of foam would never give her an edge on Lena. And you had to have something to push up before you could wear a push-up bra! So Sara had decided to get creative.

Unfortunately, sewing was not one of Sara's talents. She threw the lumpy bra on the bed. She realized that it would be a little hard to explain her sudden breast growth, anyway. *I stood a little too close to the micro-wave oven one day and they just grew.* No, that wouldn't work. The whole thing was dumb. Nicky would just have to accept her as she was. Sara slipped on her stretch bra, pulled a red T-shirt over her head, and slipped on a pair of blue jeans.

"Are you ready?" Lena stood in the hall wearing a striped cotton leotard and a short denim skirt. The outfit showed off her figure to full advantage.

"I'll be right there," Sara replied, "I'll meet you downstairs." Sara quickly ran to the bathroom, pulled out several sheets of Kleenex, and crumpled them into two small balls. She popped each wad of tissues into her bra.

Nicky and the Eggheads met, as always, down in Stingo's finished basement. The group was very proud of the microphones and amplifiers they'd bought from the money they'd made playing at school and community events. They were getting a little edgy since they hadn't had a job since they played at the Rosemont June Dance almost two months ago.

Tonight, Nicky seemed ecstatic about something when he bounded down the cellar stairs.

"Great news, everyone," he shouted. "Mike Meadows has convinced Mr. Monahan to let us play at the Hemway Day celebration at Hemway Park. It pays five hundred dollars!"

"That's one hundred dollars apiece," Sara yelled, pounding Lena on the arm excitedly.

"Congratulations," said Lena happily.

While the group cheered and discussed how they would spend the money, Sara remembered that she was supposed to work in the parking lot on Hemway Day. Mr. Meyer expected so many cars that he had arranged for two temporary toll booths to be set up in addition to Michael and Gabriel. He wanted two people at each booth, one to take money, the other to give receipt tickets. That meant all the parking lot workers had to work that day.

She didn't know what to do. She'd figure something out, she told herself.

"Let's start with 'The Beauty Inside Out,' " Nicky said, referring to the song Sara had written for the group. She'd sung it at the June dance and it had been a hit.

"I am so excited to hear you sing," Lena told Sara.

"Yeah, thanks," Sara said distractedly. She was still trying to figure out what she was going to do about Hemway Day.

Sara took her place in front of the microphone. The group played the introduction. Sara heard her cue and came in. "Make me over. Make me shout. The love inside is what it's all about. It lets the beauty inside out . . . yeah, the beauty inside out."

She knew the song well, but her mind wasn't on it. Instead she was worrying about Hemway Day. She didn't want to let the band down, but, she was surprised to discover, she felt a responsibility to her job too. Mr. Meyer was counting on her to be there. In her mind she could see Mr. Meyer hollering at her on one side, and Nicky yelling at her on the other.

Sara kept singing, "I had beauty inside of . . . hic . . . me. It took you to . . . hic . . . hic . . . hic . . . set it free."

"Wait a minute!" Nicky shouted. "Not this again. Sara, you can't get a fit of nervous hiccups every time we get a gig. Take a deep breath like I showed you."

Sara inhaled slowly, held her breath, and exhaled slowly. "I'm all right now," she said, "they're all . . . hic . . . gone."

"Sara, you were great at Rosemont," Nicky said. "There's nothing to be nervous about."

"I'm not worried about performing," Sara blurted out. "I'm . . . hic . . . worried about not being able to perform."

"What?"

Sara explained her conflict with Hemway Day. "Just quit," Nicky told her. "It's almost the end of the summer. You don't owe anything to that crazy guy Meyer."

"I do . . . hic . . . he's counting on . . . hic . . . me."

"And what about us?" Nicky shouted. "We're counting on you too. Where are we going to find a lead singer in time?"

"Excuse me," Lena spoke up. "Would your employer let me collect the money for you? I would be glad to do it."

Sara stopped and thought about it. She wished with all her heart that she could say yes, but she knew the real answer. "No, 'rules are rules'. Meyer would never go for it," she said realistically. "Thanks anyway."

"Too bad you can't sing," Nicky said to Lena.

"I can," Lena replied hesitantly.

Everyone stopped and looked at her. *Was she kidding?* Sara thought, looking around at the others. There was silence.

"All right," said Nicky, "let's see what you can do. Can you read music?"

"Ya."

"Read this then," he said, handing her the words and music to one of the group's original songs.

Sara was horror-stricken. Nicky was really going to replace her. She stood there, speechless.

"I have it," said Lena in a very short time. She walked up to the microphone. As if in a daze, Sara stepped out of the way. The group started playing their song, "Warrior."

The guitars played and Lena sang in a low, sexy voice. "I creep through the jungle. I swing through the trees. I slide on my belly and crawl on my knees. I am a warrior, warrior for your love."

She was great. Sara felt as if she couldn't breathe. How could this be happening to her? She was losing the two things that meant the most to her, Nicky and her role as lead singer, in one moment.

When Lena finished the group clapped—just as they had clapped when Sara first auditioned for them. "Now I can sing for this one time and the problem is solved," Lena said happily.

"Sing all you want," Sara shouted. "Obviously nobody cares if I'm in this band or not," she continued, staring at Nicky.

Please say you can't replace me, a voice in the center of her brain begged. *Tell me that I'm a better singer than she is.*

Everyone stared at Sara as if she'd lost her mind. In a panic, Sara turned and ran up the stairs. As she got to the door she heard Nicky running up after her. *He'll ask me to come back*, she hoped. *He'll say the band can't go on without me, that he doesn't want to lose me.*

Sara turned to face Nicky. He looked as if he were going to say all the things she longed to hear, and then his face hardened.

"You dropped something," he said, handing her the ball of wadded up Kleenex that had slipped out of her bra.

Sara was too upset to be embarrassed. Instead, she felt a strange cool calm settle over her. Without thinking about it, she reached into her shirt and pulled out the other wad of Kleenex and threw it in his face. Then she turned and ran out the door and all the way home.

Chapter Ten

"We've created a monster," Marsha stated.

"You're right," Sara agreed, "When she came here she was a total zero. We made her over, and look how she pays us back."

"She tries to steal my job, Marsha's boyfriend, and your role as singer in Nicky and the Eggheads," Rissa raged. "To think that at one time we actually felt sorry for her. Ha! That's a laugh, and the joke is on us."

The girls were sitting in Marsha's room. They were having a meeting of the Makeover Club to which Lena was most definitely *not* invited.

"I say we just ignore her altogether," Rissa continued.

"I agree," said Marsha.

"Me too," Sara agreed.

"Lena the ingrate is hereby drummed out of the Makeover Club," Marsha announced.

"Amen," shouted Sara.

On the third day of shooting the *Teen Today* commercial Rissa had finally perfected her perky persona. She felt a little dumb acting all bubbly and filled with enthusiasm over a magazine, but the director, Jed Allen, was pleased with her, and Simone Martin told her she had a strong stage presence.

Rissa found the work exciting. Since she only had

one line—"It's great to be a teen today!"—memorizing her part was no problem. For the first two days they'd walked through the movements of the scene. Jed called it blocking the scene.

Jed Allen called everyone sweetie and honey and yelled a lot, but Rissa got used to him pretty quickly. His temper tantrums weren't really any worse than those of her basketball coach, Ms. Halpern. Just as Ms. Halpern somehow got her players to move more quickly and shoot more accurately, Jed seemed to have a way—despite his shouting—of getting Rissa to do her dance and say her line with enthusiasm. "Think, Rissa," he'd coaxed. "Why is it great to be a teen today? Think of all the things that you love, and hold them in your mind when you say your line." She'd thought of her friends, and playing sports, and she'd delivered her line with feeling. "Wonderful, sweetie!" Jed had cried. "I believed you!"

Today they had shot what was called a tech rehearsal in the morning. That meant that the lighting, sound, and camera people all set up their equipment, checked levels of light and sound, and adjusted the positions of the actors accordingly. They'd done that from eight until noon. Rissa found the tech rehearsal to be the most boring part of the work.

After lunch Rissa was sent into makeup and wardrobe where a professional team made up her face and picked out an outfit for her. They had her wear a large yellow T-shirt, a purple mini, a pink oversized shirt, green socks, and yellow high-top sneakers with red laces. "Perfect," the wardrobe woman commented, sizing Rissa up. "You look like a typical teen."

I am a typical teen, thought Rissa, *and I would never dress this way.* Still, she had to admit she did look stylish and pretty.

When Rissa walked out onto the set, Simone Martin

was there. A stand-in had walked through the tech rehearsal for the actress earlier. Simone had appeared in jeans and sneakers for the two rehearsals. Now she looked gorgeous wearing a red dress with a cowl neck and swirl skirt, full makeup, and her long brown hair swept up high on her head. Simone was always friendly but businesslike. Rissa hadn't been able to tell what she was like as a person.

The commercial was filmed and it went without a hitch. "This has gone so well that we can call it a wrap," Jed announced. "Actors, you'll all be paid for the full week's work, but you're finished. Technicians, I'll see you tomorrow."

Rissa felt a sudden emptiness inside her. Was that all there was to it? No big good-byes, no round of applause—just good-bye and everyone leaves? That's exactly what happened. Simone said "Thank you all," and strode quickly out the studio door. Rissa didn't even see Jed leave. The technicians rolled up cables and secured lights within ten minutes.

The studio was soon empty and quiet. Rissa was the last one there. She stood alone on the stage. This had been a great adventure, but she hadn't been prepared for how impersonal the experience would be.

She gathered her things and took the elevator down to the lobby. There was at least a half hour before Roger was supposed to come and pick her up at six.

The sun seemed very bright to her after the cool darkness of the studio. She wandered around the block and studied the signs at Radio City Music Hall. She watched the people bustling about, all wrapped up in where they were going and who they were with. It seemed strange to be all alone with time to kill, ambling up and down this busy block.

After a while she walked back to the building where Roger was supposed to meet her. No sign of Roger.

Then she saw a familiar car parked by a fire hydrant. It was Mike's beat-up blue Mustang. She walked over to it. Mike was asleep in the front seat.

She hadn't spoken to him since they'd had their fight at the pool over her taking time off. That had been six days ago. They hadn't called each other and he hadn't come over, not even to shoot baskets with Roger as he often did.

She rapped on the window. Slowly he stirred. At first he looked as if he didn't know where he was, then he woke up and gave her a smile. He slid over into the passenger's seat and opened the door for her.

"What are you doing here?" she asked, getting into the car beside him.

"It's my day off, so I asked Roger if I could pick you up," he said, "I needed to talk to you."

Rissa looked straight out the front window. She wanted to hold him and tell him how much she'd missed him, but she didn't know what terms they were on. Maybe he'd come to tell her it was over between them.

"I want to apologize," he said. "I acted like a creep."

"No, Mike, you—"

"Let me finish, I have to say this to you. I love you. I don't want to lose you. I don't want you to . . ." his voice choked, "to outgrow me."

"I could never, Mike," she cried. "You're more important to me than anything. We always have a great time together. How could I outgrow you?"

Mike smiled sadly. "You don't see yourself the way I see you," he said. "You're going places. You're beautiful. You have spirit. You're strong and you're smart."

"I'm not," she said, "I'm not any of those things. I just love you." She'd never said that to him before, but the words came easily.

He pulled her to him and wrapped his arms around her. "You're all those things, and much more," he said. "And the more I know you, the more I can't believe a plain guy like me will be able to hold you. I don't want you to become rich and famous and forget all about me, but I can't hold you down either. If I do that, then we both lose."

Something in his voice made Rissa look up at him. His lashes were glistening. Were there tears in his eyes?

They sat in the car holding each other for a long time. "I'm done with the commercial," she said after a while.

"Great," he said. "How did you like it?"

"I'm not sure," she answered truthfully. "It was very exciting, and they paid me a lot of money, plus I'm going to get one hundred dollars every time it's on TV. It was a great opportunity."

"Then what aren't you sure about?"

"It was so cold, somehow. It was as if nobody saw me, Rissa. All they saw was a girl saying some lines. Once I stopped saying my lines, it was like I wasn't even there anymore as far as the other people were concerned. Everyone seemed so wrapped up in themselves. It was lonely."

He held her tighter to him. "Don't worry. I won't let you be lonely. Not if I can help it."

Rissa smiled and hugged Mike in return. She had the strange but wonderful feeling of having come home after having been away a long time.

The house was quiet when Rissa got home. At first, she thought no one was there, but when she walked into the kitchen she saw that her father was sitting at the table. He hadn't heard her come in. She looked at him for a second. His leathery, deep-lined face looked sad. She saw that he was studying the picture of her mother that usually stood on the living room end table.

"Hi, Dad," she said softly.

He looked up, startled. "Hi," he answered, seeming to study Rissa's face. "I hadn't realized how much you've gotten to look like your mother," he said finally.

Rissa sat down beside her father and looked at the photo. Funny, she'd never noticed it before, either, but she did look like her mother. She had the same eyes and the same smile. Her mother was smiling in this picture.

"She looks happy," Rissa commented.

Her father smiled at her. "I think she was happy with our life together and with you children," he said. "I know I was."

The word "was" echoed in Rissa's head. "Are you happy now, Dad?" she asked.

"I don't know," he answered. "I go to my job. I take care of my family. I'm glad we're all healthy and we don't have any big problems." He knocked on the wooden table superstitiously. "I guess that should make me happy, but . . ."

"But it's not enough?"

"It's enough, but, I guess every person needs to be . . . seen. Maybe that makes no sense."

"Does Mary see you?"

Her father looked surprised by the question. "I think she does," he answered slowly. "You didn't take to Mary, did you?"

"I suppose we didn't get off to a good start," Rissa admitted, "but I'll try to be more friendly to her if it would make you happy."

"It would make me happy," he said, hugging her to his side. "And you know what? You make me happy."

Chapter Eleven

Lena continued her eight o'clock swims—alone. Rissa, who usually joined her, had joined Sara and Marsha in giving Lena the cold shoulder.

A single lifeguard was assigned to watch as Lena and three other swimmers did their rigorous morning workouts, back and forth, back and forth, in the roped-off lanes. The rhythmic breathing and hard stroking required for the swim helped Lena relax and think more clearly. Today, she had a lot to think about.

For the first time in her life she looked and felt prettier than she'd ever dreamed possible. Yet she'd never felt more confused. Her friends, Sara, Marsha, and Rissa, hadn't spoken to her in three days. Sara spoke only when spoken to and spent the time at home alone in her room.

What had she done that was so terrible? She'd just tried to be friendly and helpful. Maybe it had been some of the same old problem in a new form. Maybe she was still trying too hard. *Think first, talk second,* she scolded herself.

Still, she couldn't help but feel that she'd been treated unfairly. It was hard to feel accepted by three friends and then be shut out. It hurt.

Lena stopped at the edge of the pool and lifted herself, panting, up onto its side. Her body needed a break, but her mind was racing. Tad would be coming to work soon. She was surprised at how much she looked forward to seeing him.

Mike had kept her on as a junior lifeguard even after Rissa returned to work. Working at the pool was a lot of fun and being alongside Tad made it doubly so. Tad had such a bright, handsome smile, and he smiled at Lena quite a bit. He was unashamedly enchanted with her. No one had ever admired her before, certainly no handsome boy.

Lena pushed off the side of the pool. She tried to do twenty-five laps a day—five more to go. As her lean body cut through the water, she thought of all the new friends she'd made at the pool. She should be feeling wonderful. She was suddenly pretty and popular. She even had a job. Why should she let three jealous girls get her down?

She sputtered and had to come up for air. Jealous? She'd never even thought about it before. Was it possible they'd snubbed her because they envied her. Her? Lena?

No, not possible, she told herself. Lena's image of herself hadn't yet caught up to her new self. She couldn't imagine anyone being jealous of her.

Lena climbed out of the pool and grabbed her towel off the chair. She forgot her uncomfortable thoughts the minute she saw Tad walking down the ramp toward her.

"You are up early," she commented cheerfully.

"I just wanted to say hi before work started. I know you always work out in the morning."

They chatted about pool gossip until Lena noticed that it was almost nine. She had to go up to the locker room to put on a dry suit and her blue pool shorts. "I will see you in a few moments." She excused herself.

On the way into the locker room she was surprised

to see Doris coming out. Doris usually didn't show up at the pool until noon.

"Just the person I wanted to see," Doris said sweetly.

Lena checked over her shoulder, sincerely thinking that Doris must be talking to someone else. There was no one behind her. Involuntarily, Lena backed up a few steps away from Doris. Experience had made her wary of the other girl.

"I want to bury the hatchet," Doris said. Lena had never heard the expression and half-expected to swing around and see Craig or Heather coming at her with a hatchet. She tensed for a moment, but when nothing happened she took a breath.

"I do not understand," she said honestly.

"I want to be friends," Doris continued. "I know I haven't always been so nice to you, but I'm sorry. I don't always take well to new people. Can we be friends?"

Lena was speechless. After a few moments she said, "Yes, I suppose so."

"That's fabulous!" Doris trilled, giving Lena's arm a friendly squeeze. "I can't wait to introduce you to all my friends. Would you like to come to my house after your shift? My mother will pick us up. When should I tell her to come?"

"My shift is over at one," Lena said, still leery of the situation.

"Great, then you can come over and stay for dinner," Doris said. "I'm going to take a swim. See you down at the pool."

Doris crinkled up her nose and treated Lena to one of her most winning smiles. Then she ran off to the pool. Lena ran her hand through her fine blonde hair. Things were changing so fast.

* * *

"You are not going to believe this," Sara told Marsha over the phone. "Guess where Lena is tonight."

"Out with Tad Baker."

"No."

"I don't know, off being Miss Perfect somewhere."

"She is sleeping over at Doris Gaylord's house."

"Have you flipped?"

"I'm telling you the truth. Ask Rissa. She saw Lena get into Doris's mother's Jaguar. Lena just called to ask if she could sleep over."

"This is too disgusting for words," groaned Marsha. "Even if we weren't already mad at her, we couldn't be friends with her now. How could she? Yuck!"

"I thought Doris hated Lena," said Sara, "especially since Tad hasn't looked at her since the *new* Lena showed up."

Marsha thought for a moment. It *was* odd. What was Doris up to? "It makes sense in a way, if you stop to think about it," she said. "We know Tad is goofy over Lena. If Doris is friendly with Lena, she'll also see a lot of Tad. When Lena goes home in two weeks, guess who'll be left behind to take her place."

"Doris."

"I'll bet you anything that's what Doris is up to."

"We should warn Lena," said Sara.

"Did you forget? We're not speaking to her."

"Oh, yeah." After Sara hung up she began to think about her feud with Lena. It suddenly seemed petty. She missed talking to her. She even missed that stupid, snorting laugh. Then she remembered that Lena would be singing with Nicky and the Eggheads. And she remembered that Nicky hadn't called her since their fight—and her heart hardened.

The next day, Marsha was on her way to the baby-sitting center when she noticed about ten girls gathered

95

around the bulletin board. She jumped up in an effort to see over their heads, but she couldn't. "What's going on?" she asked a girl in front of her.

"They're holding a Junior Miss Hemway Park beauty contest on Hemway Day," the girl explained. "You have to be fourteen to eighteen, and the contestants are limited to the first twenty-five girls to sign up. First prize is two hundred dollars!"

Marsha knew she wasn't a beauty queen, but Rissa was. There wasn't time to ask her if she wanted to enter the contest. The list was filling up fast. Marsha knew she had to sign Rissa up.

She wriggled her way to the front of the group and in a few minutes she had hold of the pencil on a string that dangled next to the sign-up sheet.

Marsha penciled Rissa's name on the list. She was just in time—there were only two blank spaces after her name. Marsha took another minute to scan the list of names for any that might be familiar to her. Two of the assistants from the baby-sitting center where there. *Cute, but no real competition,* Marsha assessed. There was another girl listed whom Marsha knew from school. *Also good-looking, but Rissa has a better figure.* As her eyes traveled to the top of the list she saw two more names she knew.

In even, angular handwriting she saw the name Lena Laffleberger. Just below it, in big loopy writing was the name Doris Gaylord, the i in Doris dotted with a heart.

"What do you mean you would never be in a beauty contest?" Marsha shouted.

"It's too dumb. It's icky," Rissa told her. "Hand me that blue marker, please."

Rissa and Marsha were in the small lifeguards' office. Marsha had finished her baby-sitting shift and had come up to talk to her friend. Rissa had been assigned to make up signs announcing the Hemway Day events.

"Nicky and the Eggheads appearing at the bandshell at six," she read out loud as she carefully printed the words. "What a gyp that Sara can't sing with them. I can't believe Nicky is being such a little jerk and using Lena instead. They should have just turned down the job."

"He cares about Nicky and the Eggheads more than anything in the world, it seems," remarked Marsha. "I suppose he cares about it more than he cares about Sara's feelings . . . hey, you spelled unique wrong."

"Let's get back to the beauty contest. I think you should enter the contest. You could win it. You're a model. Besides, it has a two hundred-dollar prize."

Rissa looked interested for the first time, so Marsha pressed her case. "Doris and Lena have signed up, too. Do you want to see either of them win? Wouldn't that just bug the life out of you?"

Rissa looked almost convinced, but then she went back to her sign. "It's too late, anyway. I heard the sheet filled up inside an hour."

At that minute Mr. Monahan entered the office. "So, Miss Lupinski," he said to Rissa, "I was glad to see you signed up for the Miss Hemway contest. You surprised me. I didn't think that was your style. It shows real Hemway spirit. Makes the pool staff look like they're really cooperating."

"But, Mr. Mona—" Rissa began.

"I know, I know," he said gathering papers out of his desk drawer. "Lena signed up too. Nice of you not to hog all the credit. I think it's great that you girls have a sense of healthy competition, but you can still be friends. I admire that, and I won't forget it when it comes to picking staff for next summer."

Mr. Monahan clipped his papers onto his clipboard and gathered up the finished signs. "Just think, you could be the first Junior Miss Hemway," he said, patting her on the shoulder and bounding out the door.

Rissa threw down her marker in disgust. "Now what am I going to do? When he finds out I didn't sign up for the contest he's going to think Lena is the only one with *Hemway spirit*."

"You did sign up for the contest," Marsha informed her, twirling a pencil between her fingers smugly. "You can thank me later."

Rissa just buried her head in her hands and groaned.

Chapter Twelve

Marsha and Jim had been to a six o'clock movie. They walked home hand in hand. "It's starting to get dark," Jim commented. "It's hard to believe the summer's almost over."

"Mmmmmm," Marsha agreed absently. Her mind was on other things. She knew in her heart that summer wasn't the only thing that was ending.

A block before her house, Jim stopped and leaned against a tree to tie his shoelace. She stood next to him and in another minute they were kissing.

The truth Marsha didn't want to face was increasingly clear to her. The feeling that had inspired their last kiss wasn't love, it was competition. She didn't want to lose Jim to Lena. But that wasn't fair to him.

She pulled away from him gently and looked into his face. His green eyes looked all dreamy and romantic, but it was no use pretending she felt the same way. It just wasn't true.

"Jim," she began, "I have to talk to you about something. It's kind of hard to discuss." An expression of worry clouded his face. He pushed off from the tree and started to walk again, his hands jammed into his pockets.

"You know I like you a lot, a whole lot," she continued, walking alongside him. "It's just that—"

He stopped and faced her. This was going to be so hard to do. "I think we had a better time as friends than we're having as boyfriend and girlfriend," she finished.

Jim looked at her blankly, as if he didn't quite understand what she meant. Then his brow creased into a deep scowl. "Fine," he said angrily.

"I hope we can stay friends," she added, meekly.

"I don't think so, Marsha. I don't feel very friendly toward you right now. How long have you been stringing me along?"

"That's not fair!" Marsha cried. "We've only been going together since June. It took time to figure out how I felt."

"I knew how I felt all long," he replied.

"Well, I'm sorry, but it didn't seem so simple to me."

Marsha wanted to run and hide. Her stomach was doing flip-flops. She reached out to touch his arm soothingly, but he yanked it away. Marsha thought she saw tears in his eyes. "I don't think we can be friends," he said brusquely, turning and hurrying down the block.

Marsha stood there a moment, shaking. She walked the rest of the way to her house feeling empty inside.

Her mother and father were sitting in the living room reading the paper when she came in. "What's wrong?" her mother asked immediately. "You're so pale."

The concern in her mother's voice shattered Marsha's calm facade. "I broke up with Jim," she said, bursting into tears. "I've hurt him so badly. He hates me now."

Marsha's mother was on her feet and hugging her in seconds. Marsha held her mother tightly and cried into her shoulder. When her tears subsided, her father held out the box of tissues he'd gotten from the bathroom.

"You're too young to be going steady, anyway," he said, trying to be helpful.

"Maybe," she said through her sniffles. How could she explain to him how great it was to have a boyfriend, someone who liked you better than any other girl? And her father would never understand how awful it felt to see the look of hurt on Jim's face and to know she had put it there.

"Did you two have a fight?" her mother asked, stroking her hair the way she'd done when Marsha was small.

"No, I just feel more friendly than girlfriendly toward Jim and it didn't seem right to go on acting as if I felt a way that I don't. I did the right thing, didn't I?"

"It sounds like it," her mother agreed. "It sounds to me like you did a very honorable thing."

"Honorable?" Marsha questioned. "I feel terrible. I tried to feel differently toward Jim. I don't understand why I couldn't. He's so nice and sweet."

"The chemistry between two people is one of the most mysterious things in the world," commented her father. "The world is full of nice, sweet people who are wonderful to know, but why we fall in love with one over all the others is pretty hard to explain."

"It will happen to you someday," her mother added. "This just wasn't it, and you were right not to pretend. Don't feel guilty. Jim will get over this."

"I don't think so, Mom. You should have seen his face."

"His pride is hurt, and he's disappointed, but he'll recover. You haven't inflicted a mortal wound. You may feel that you've been cruel now, but in the long run, you did the kind thing."

"I think I'll just lie down in my room for awhile," she said, smiling at her parents weakly. "What you've said makes sense, but I still feel like I stabbed a good friend."

Lena had never seen a home as lavish as Doris's. She could barely keep her jaw from dropping in amazement when she first saw the large brick home standing on the top of a large sloping lawn. Doris's mother had opened the garage door electronically and pulled her hunter green Jaguar into the spacious two-car garage. A door from the garage led directly into the house.

Lena had been impressed by the large sunken pool just outside the sliding glass patio doors. Doris brought Lena up to her bedroom. The room itself was decorated in a pink floral pattern. Everything matched—the curtains, the bedspread, even the canopy over Doris's bed. This was the kind of room Lena had thought existed only in magazines or on TV.

After their swim in the backyard pool, the maid had brought them snacks outside on the patio. Dinner was served by the maid in the elegant dining room.

Lena had felt uncomfortable when Doris's mother and father started to squabble in the middle of dinner over a weekend trip they'd been invited on. Her father had stormed away from the table in a huff when Doris's mother refused to discuss the weekend with him any further.

Lena had felt terrible for Doris. "Would you like me to go home?" she had asked. "Perhaps this is not a good time for a visit."

"Because of Mommy and Daddy?" Doris asked, astonished. "Don't worry about them. That's just how they are."

Lena and Doris had watched a movie starring Tom Cruise on the VCR hooked up to the wide-screen TV in Doris's den. Then they'd headed up to bed.

Doris had nothing but compliments for Lena all night long. She was so funny, so pretty, so unique, Doris told her. Lena was thrilled to hear this rich, popular girl singing her praises. She could hardly believe this was the same girl who'd been so mean to her.

Doris lent Lena one of her father's undershirts to sleep in and finally, at about two in the morning, the girls had settled down to sleep in Doris's queen-sized bed. It was a warm night but the air conditioner in Doris's room made it feel good to snuggle down under the quilt.

When the lights were out, Doris had started asking Lena question after question about Tad Baker. Surely, she thought, eventually Lena would reveal something she could use against her. But no luck. Doris decided to try again the next day.

In the next two days Doris never left Lena's side. She'd insisted that they sign up together for the Junior Miss Hemway Park beauty contest. Doris took Lena shopping and treated her to some accessories. On the third day she threw a small pool party and invited Lena. "Invite Tad too," she suggested casually.

"I will, Doris," Lena agreed. "We will have a wonderful time."

Sara snapped a tape into her Walkman. This Whitney Houston tape always cheered her up. She hoped it would work now, because she was down in the dumps.

It had been five days since their fight, and Nicky still hadn't called her. She lay flat on her bed and let the music spill into her ears. The music did make her feel better.

This waiting is making me nuts, she said to herself. *There's no reason why I can't call him.* She went into her mother's room and called Nicky.

"Hello," his husky accented voice greeted her.

"It's me, Sara."

"Sara!" he cried happily, and then as if suddenly remembering that they were fighting, added, "How have you been?" more coolly.

"Not great," she admitted. "I'd like to see you."

In a half an hour, Sara was entering Frank's Pizzeria in the center of Rosemont, where they'd agreed to meet. She bought a slice and a soda and then slipped into one of the red plastic booths.

She glanced at her image in the marbleized mirrored paneling along the walls. She noticed that the roots of her dyed hair needed a touch-up. She ran her fingers through her hair to fluff the soft curls up higher on her head. She straightened her oversized aqua tank top.

She saw Nicky come in and look around. It seemed to her that he'd also taken extra care with his appearance. He wore a large blue-striped sports shirt that he knew she liked.

He spotted her and smiled nervously. Sliding into the seat across from her, he immediately fell to playing with the paper wrapper from Sara's straw.

"How's Lena doing with the songs?" Sara asked.

"We haven't had a rehearsal since the last one you were at. She's supposed to be learning them though."

"Oh," she said, disappointed that he hadn't changed his mind about letting Lena sing.

They stared at one another nervously for a long minute. "Are we breaking up or not?" Sara blurted out finally. "Were we ever going together?" she continued. "It's kind of hard to tell if you're going out with someone who never asks you on a date, or holds your hand, or calls you about anything besides songs and rehearsals."

Nicky looked surprised. "Can't you tell how I feel?"

Sara leaned in toward him. "The few times you

kissed me, I thought I knew how you felt, but then that's it. You don't do anything else that's, you know, boyfriendish.''

"Does it have to have a label?'' he protested. "Can't we just care about each other?''

"Do you care about me?''

Nicky looked embarrassed. "Can't you tell I do?''

"No, I can't,'' Sara told him. "You made me feel as if it didn't matter to you at all if I left the group. It wasn't like it was my fault. I feel terrible about it. Do you think I'd rather collect stupid old parking fees than sing with the Eggheads?''

"I told you to quit.''

"On the biggest day of the year?'' she protested. "Meyer thinks I'm a flake anyway and I can't bear to prove him right. Besides, you didn't even give me a chance to think about it. You just stuck Lena right in my place.''

"Wait a minute,'' Nicky argued. "Lena was only trying to help and it seemed like a good solution. It was you who got all bent out of shape. Nobody said anything about you not singing with the Eggheads for good.''

Sara had to admit that what he said was true. "That Lena just bugs me,'' she mumbled. "You didn't even like her until we fixed her up, and now you can't take your eyes off her jiggling around on the diving board.''

Nicky blushed for a second. "I guess you really don't know how I feel about you,'' he said thoughtfully. He stared at her and then got up abruptly and walked out of the pizzeria.

Sara was stunned. Why had he just left? Now she was really confused.

In the next minute Nicky returned. His attitude had changed. He was smiling and energetic. "I'm the new Nicky,'' he said cheerfully as he slid into the booth next to her. "I'm going to tell you exactly how I feel. I would like you to be my girlfriend. I hope you come back to sing with Nicky and the Eggheads after your career as a parking fee taker ends. And I love the way you look, every inch of you. Now do you know how I feel?"

"Am I a better singer than she is?" Sara asked.

"Not so much better as different," he replied. Sara narrowed her eyes at him. "Yes," he laughed, "on second thought, you are much better. Decidedly superior."

"When will we go on a date?" she asked.

"Tomorrow, at five o'clock. I'm taking you to Kelly's Diner for supper. Sorry it's not fancier, but some of us weren't lucky enough to get a summer job."

Sara threw her arms around his neck. She kissed him on the nose and on the forehead. "My boyfriend," she said happily, then she kissed him on the lips with a loud smack.

Chapter Thirteen

"Tell the girls the hot piece of gossip you told me," Roger said to Mike. Mike was driving Rissa, Roger, Sara, and Marsha to Hemway Park on Hemway Day.

"Naw," Mike said. "I don't want to."

"Tell! Tell!" cried Marsha and Sara from the backseat.

"Okay," Mike relented. "I was talking to Tad the other day and he told me that he went to a pool party at Doris's house with Lena."

"That's no gossip," Sara moaned. "I could have told you that. Lena said the party was *wunderbar*. Who cares?"

"Let him finish," Roger told her.

"The gossip part is that while Lena was around, Doris and her pal Heather pretended to think Lena was the wonder of the ages, but Doris maneuvered it so that Tad had to drive her into town for more ice. When they were alone in the car, she started coming on strong to him, telling him that Lena was only using him for a summer fling, and that she had lots of guys on the string. Then Doris started sitting real close to him in the car."

"This is great," Rissa chuckled. "Then what?"

"He told her to get lost."

"Yeaaaa!" cheered Sara and Marsha.

"He told me that he told Doris off and said he

intended to write to Lena and hoped to get to Switzerland next summer."

"Wow, the guy is serious," Rissa commented, impressed.

"I knew it! I knew it!" shouted Marsha. "Doris was only looking for a way to get next to Tad. That girl is so mean."

"Excuse me for saying so, but don't you think you guys have been pretty mean to Lena too?" said Roger. "It's not her fault that she's the most beautiful, talented, wonderful girl on the face of the earth."

"She is not," shouted Rissa, punching her brother hard on the arm.

"We're not like Doris," added Sara. "We have good reasons for being mad at her."

"If you say so," replied Roger, unconvinced.

Roger's remarks had struck home. How good were their reasons, really? Marsha had been angered because Jim seemed to prefer Lena to her. Why shouldn't he have preferred a girl who was making a fuss over him to one who was giving him only half her attention? Sara and Rissa both privately admitted to themselves that their anger had been based on jealousy. These thoughts were painful, because in her own way, each of the girls prided herself on being kind and fair.

"Well, I don't like her anyway," stated Marsha flatly, pushing the annoying guilt pangs from her head. "Any friend of Doris Gaylord's is no friend of mine."

"That's right," agreed Sara weakly.

"She deserves whatever she gets," insisted Rissa with less than her usual conviction.

For the rest of the ride the girls chattered about the beauty contest. "I still say it's dumb," said Rissa, but her friends could tell that the spirit of competition had gotten into Rissa once again. Rissa always played to win.

"Is your dad going to come and see you in the contest?" Mike asked.

"Are you joking?" said Rissa. "He'd come to a swim meet, but a beauty contest, never."

"Doris is going to die," gloated Sara. "First you beat her at the *Teen Today* contest and now you're going to beat her at this."

"I hope so," said Rissa, fighting a wave of nerves and insecurity.

"I'm going to miss it all," moaned Sara. "I'll be stuck in that stupid parking lot the whole day."

As Mr. Meyer had predicted, the lines of cars streaming into the lot for Hemway Day seemed never ending. Sara felt like a human ticket dispenser, handing out orange, blue, and yellow tickets without a break. She was coupled with Merry Meyer in Gabriel for Mr. Meyer's special emergency two-in-a-booth strategy. Having Sara beside her seemed to calm Merry's nerves. She only spent twenty minutes in the ladies' room the entire morning.

By three o'clock the cars had tapered down to a trickle and the parking lot was almost entirely full. Mr. Meyer came out and observed his booths critically. "Everyone arrived earlier than I expected," he mumbled, half to himself and half to Merry and Sara. "I can afford to let some of this staff go home early."

Sara smiled at him eagerly. "Merry, you leave," he told his daughter.

Merry brightened, but noticing Sara's crestfallen expression, she hesitated. "I can stay, Daddy," she said. "I don't mind."

"If we get another rush, do you think you can handle it?" he asked skeptically.

"Daddy," Merry answered indignantly. "I'm a Meyer. Parking lots are in my blood."

Mr. Meyer smiled at his daughter proudly. "That's my girl! All right, Miss Marshall, you can go."

Squealing with delight, Sara kissed Merry on the cheek. "This is for all the times you covered for me," Merry whispered.

Sara ran up the stairs toward the ladies' locker room to see if she could find Marsha or Rissa. The contest was set for three-thirty. By three-fifteen, most of the contestants were ready and waiting around in the area by the pool ramp.

Sara hurried into the locker room. No Rissa or Marsha. They must be outside already. Sara dashed into the ladies' room for one last check before heading toward the pool.

While she was in one of the ladies' room stalls, Sara heard two very familiar voices in the bathroom with her. They belonged to Doris and Heather. Sara stayed where she was and listened to what they were saying.

"Have you got everything?" she heard Doris ask.

"It's all here in the bag," Heather assured her. "I think I remembered everything you told me to bring."

"Let's see. A dinner plate, good. A candle. Matches. And peppermints. Good work," Doris said, sounding delighted.

Sara heard the snap of a match on the flint paper and smelled a smoky odor. There was a minute or two of silence broken only by intermittent fits of giggling from Doris and Heather.

"Now put the peppermints on the plate," Doris instructed. "This is going to be a riot. I can't wait to see Tad Baker's face when he sees this."

Heather and Doris scurried out of the room. Sara couldn't imagine what they were up to. Rotten as Doris was, Sara didn't think she'd try to hurt Tad or Lena with a poison peppermint. What then?

Sara ran out of the ladies' room. She shaded her eyes

from the bright sun and saw Rissa and Marsha standing in the area outside the locker rooms with the contestants. She ran over to join them. Marsha was busy fussing with Rissa's hair, trying to spray down a curl that was sticking out in the wrong direction.

"How is this going to work?" Sara asked.

"The contestants wait up here until they hear their names called, and then each contestant walks down the ramp to the platform that's been set up by the pool," Rissa told her.

Sara walked to the head of the ramp and looked down to the pool area. At the bottom of the ramp a wooden platform had been set up beside the pool. A table of judges sat on the ramp and a microphone stood in the middle of the platform. The pool chairs had been arranged all around the ramp and the platform.

Sara walked back to her friends and told them what she'd heard in the ladies' room. "I don't know what Doris is planning," remarked Marsha, "but I bet it's aimed at Lena."

The girls looked around and caught sight of Lena looking down the ramp nervously at the crowd below her. She'd shed the last few pounds she needed to lose, and the electric blue suit they'd persuaded her to buy had never looked better on her. Her hair had been bleached a shade lighter from the sun, and her golden tan made her blue eyes sparkle.

"I think she's wearing too much makeup," Marsha commented.

"Who are you kidding?" said Rissa. "She looks gorgeous."

"You look gorgeous too," said Sara. Rissa was wearing a red floral print one-piece suit with a high, square neckline and a low back. She'd set her hair so that it tousled gently around her face. She also had a deep tan that set off her eyes to their best advantage.

"She looks pretty good too," Rissa said sourly, pointing to Doris. Doris's shoulder length hair had been set in a million small curls that cascaded around her shoulders. Her yellow bikini fit her so well it looked as if it had been made specifically for her.

"What's Heather doing?" asked Marsha, watching as Heather circulated through the crowd offering peppermints to the contestants.

"It's the poison mints, or whatever, that I told you about," said Sara urgently. "I wish I could figure out what's going on."

There was a crackle of static from the microphone. The county superintendent of parks was addressing the crowd that filled the seats in the pool area. "I want to welcome you to this, our very first Hemway Day celebration," he announced.

He went on to tell about different park programs and what they hoped to accomplish in the coming years. Rissa and Marsha listened, but Sara kept craning her neck over to see what Doris and Heather were up to. She noticed that they'd taken Lena over into a corner in the far end of the area where the contestants waited. Heather and Doris seemed to be explaining something to Lena, who smiled and nodded.

The speaker on the platform changed. Now Mr. Monahan was introducing the judges and explaining to the crowd the rules of the Junior Miss Hemway Park contest. The girls would be judged not only on looks, but on poise and on their response to a question put to them by the judges.

Sara checked back over her shoulder and saw that Lena had joined Doris and Heather in a corner near the entrance to the locker room. Doris seemed to be performing some strange ritual. Her eyes were closed and she was rubbing her fingers all over her face. "What on earth?" Sara muttered to herself.

Mr. Monahan called for the girls to line up in alphabetical order, as they'd been shown earlier, and to walk down the ramp when he read out their names.

Sara crept closer to Lena, whose back was now turned to her. Lena seemed to be going through the same strange face rubbing ritual as Doris had done.

"Oh, lucky mints bring luck. Lucky mints bring me luck. Lucky mints bring me luck. I wipe the luck all around me," Sara heard Lena say.

Lucky mints? Sara noticed Doris and Heather quickly exchange laughing glances. "Have to go now," Doris said. She rushed over to the ramp entrance just as the judge called "Doris Gaylord."

Sara watched as Doris strode confidently down the ramp. When she turned her attention back to Lena, she was horrified. "Lena, what happened!" she cried.

Lena gave her a big smile. She had no idea that her face was covered with black smudges. She looked as if she'd fallen into a coal bin. "Doris told me that in America you rub a plate of peppermints for good luck and then rub your face, so the luck will rub off on you," Lena told her.

"That's not luck you have all over your face," said Sara. Sara picked up the plate that Heather had set off to the side before she disappeared down into the pool area. The bottom of it was covered with black soot.

Rissa and Marsha had noticed what happened and had rushed over. "We used to play this trick at parties," Marsha said, when saw what had happened. "You burn a candle under a plate and it makes all this ashy, sooty stuff. Then you pretend to wipe the bottom of the plate and rub your face, but you know the stuff is there, so you don't really rub the plate. The other person doesn't know so they get covered with it."

"Oh, no!" cried Lena, looking into the pocket mirror Marsha had handed her. "I might have walked out there like this. Everyone would have thought I had lost my mind."

Sara came running out of the ladies' locker room holding a wad of wet paper towels. She dabbed at Lena's face. The darn stuff wouldn't come off. All she was managing to do was smear Lena's mascara down her cheeks.

Rissa pulled Lena toward the ladies' room. "We have to wash your face, quick."

"There is no time," wailed Lena.

At that moment Nicky and Jim came out of the men's locker room. Marsha ran up to Jim. "I need your towel," she told him urgently. He hadn't intended to ever speak to Marsha again, but the tone of her voice made him forget he was mad at her.

"What's the matter?" he asked.

Marsha pointed to Lena. "I'll explain later," she said. She soaked Jim's towel in the water fountain and went back to work on Lena's face.

Nicky pulled Sara aside. "Are you off?" he asked. She nodded. "Do you want to sing?"

Sara thought a moment. "How about if I sing some songs with Lena?" she asked. "We can talk later. Right now I have to figure a way to get this black smeary stuff off her face."

Nicky rummaged through the gym bag he was carrying and pulled out a white bag of fried chicken. "I have these wet napkin things I got with my order of chicken," he offered.

"Miss Lena Laffleberger," they heard Mr. Monahan call.

"Don't panic," Marsha assured Lena, tearing open the foil pouch of the wet napkin Nicky had handed her. "Jim, run down and ask them to put Lena last. Please."

"Sure thing."

"Thanks," she said sincerely.

"Always glad to help out my friends," he told her as he ran off. Jim ran down the ramp, causing a round of laughter in the audience. He apparently gave his message because Mr. Monahan went on to the next name.

"Rissa Lupinski." Rissa was busy scrubbing Lena's forehead with a paper towel. "Rissa Lupinski," she heard them announce again. "Oh, Miss Lupinski," Mr. Monahan called for the third time.

"Go! Go!" Sara urged her friend. "We'll take care of this."

Casting worried glances over her shoulder, Rissa rushed off toward the ramp. Halfway down she reminded herself to stop running and attempted to look poised. She looked out over the audience and forced herself to smile through her nervousness. She walked up the four steps to the ramp and shook hands with Mr. Monahan as she'd been instructed to do.

She walked to both corners of the platform and then took her place on line with the other contestants. She was only five girls away from Doris who was smiling effervescently. It was hard for Rissa to smile while thinking how much she'd like to reach over and smash the petite girl, but she managed to anyway. "The show must go on," Rissa thought, and she smiled.

Mr. Monahan went through the alphabet until he'd introduced a girl with the last name of Zweibel, then he called Lena's name. Rissa squinted into the bright sunlight, trying to look up the ramp. There was no sign of Lena.

Mr. Monahan called her name three times. "I guess Miss Laffleberger was unavoidably delayed," Mr. Monahan said. "Now to the next part of our contest . . ."

Chapter Fourteen

"I am coming!" said Lena, her words taking on a heavy accent, which was a sure sign that she was nervous. "Here I am." Rissa saw her trotting down the ramp, her long legs carrying her quickly.

"No need to rush, Miss Laffleberger, we can wait," Mr. Monahan said kindly. Rissa watched as Lena walked the platform and did her turns. She noticed that her face was a bit red from scrubbing and her hair was slightly wet, but Marsha and Sara had done a good job of hastily reapplying her makeup and—all things considered—she looked only slightly the worse for her near-calamity.

Rissa noticed that Doris tensed and then dropped her shoulders in frustration. She hadn't eliminated or embarrassed Lena after all.

Lena joined the other contestants in the line. "Let's have a hand for our brave contestants," Mr. Monahan urged the audience.

As the audience applauded, Rissa again squinted her eyes against the blinding sunlight and looked out into the crowd. Her smile brightened at what she saw. There in the first row sat her father. Beside him was Mary, smiling and clapping.

Rissa caught her father's eye. He nodded and gave

her a thumb's-up sign. She flashed a quick thumb's-up back to him.

"For the next part of our contest, the judges have prepared one question which all the girls will have a chance to answer," Mr. Monahan announced. The judges will evaluate the girls' responses on the basis of sincerity, expressiveness, and poise. Here is the question: What do you value most about your friends?"

Rissa's mind raced. What would she say? She squinted again and caught sight of Marsha, Sara, Nicky, and Jim standing together off to the side of the platform. What did they mean to her? She couldn't picture life without them. How could she express that in a few words?

She looked around some more. In another corner she saw Roger and Mike standing together. They both had their arms folded seriously, as if this were a matter of life or death. They cared so much about her. They wanted her to win if it made her happy. Roger was her brother and Mike was her boyfriend—but they both counted as friends too.

And then there was Mary. Maybe she'd turn out to be a friend after awhile. She was here today, wasn't she? That counted for something.

Rissa was glad she didn't have to answer first. Some of the girls said they valued loyalty, a sense of humor, good advice. Rissa certainly valued those things too. She saw those qualities in her friends.

She glanced back at Lena, standing at the end of the line. Lena had bailed her out when she needed the week off. It was only her own jealousy and insecurity that had blinded her to Lena's good intentions. She had to face that. She promised herself to apologize as soon as she had the chance.

Rissa heard Doris speaking. "Friends are people

who are a lot like you are" she said. "They should be witty, attractive, and always willing to help me. The thing I value most in my friends is the many things they do for me."

A burst of applause rang out from the section where Doris's friends were seated. "All right, Doris!" cheered Heather.

She gets my vote for sincerity on that one, thought Rissa. *If you can do something for Doris, she'll like you fine.*

A few more girls spoke, then it was Rissa's turn. Her mind went blank. She coughed nervously. She looked down at her father. He looked worried that she'd freeze up. He'd seen her freeze at a big basketball game last year when she played center. Thinking about how well he knew her brought an idea into Rissa's head.

"All the things the other girls have mentioned today—humor, sincerity, loyalty—are all important to me," she began, "but I think the thing I value most about my friends is that they know me, with all my faults, and my fears, and they're still my friends. Someone I love very much said to me recently that it's important to feel that at least one person in the world sees you. *You*, your real, true self, as you really are. I'm lucky that I have a few people who see me and care about me. Sometimes we get so wrapped up in our own concerns that we don't see the people around us clearly. If I can give anything back to people, I hope it's that I take the time to see the real them."

A loud clap came from Mike which was immediately taken up by the audience. "Yeaaa!" cheered Sara and Marsha. Nicky whistled through his fingers to show his support.

"We see you brought your cheering section with you

118

today," said Mr. Monahan, chuckling. Rissa blushed and took her place back on line.

The last contestant to answer the question was Lena. She stepped to the microphone and cleared her throat. "I have learned that friends can have misunderstandings," she said. "Friends can even be angry at one another. But, to me, friends are those people who do not abandon you when you need help, no matter what small arguments you have had in the past. We all do things that annoy one another, but friends overlook that when it comes time to help."

"Bravo!" yelled Tad Baker from the audience, jumping to his feet.

Marsha, Sara, Jim, and Nicky joined him. "Bravo!" they yelled together. The rest of the audience clapped along with them.

"Another cheering section," joked Mr. Monahan. "Thank you, Lena. Now if you will join the other girls for one final walk around the stage, the judges will then cast their ballots for Junior Miss Hemway Park."

The girls walked around the platform one more time, then resumed their original spots and waited. After a few minutes, Mr. Monahan returned to the microphone.

"In my eyes, all these girls are winners," he said. "It takes guts to come up here in front of all these people. But the judges have made their decision and without further ado, let me announce our finalists."

The contestants shuffled nervously. Lena caught Rissa's eye. She mouthed the words, "Good luck."

"The fourth runner-up is . . . Miss Doris Gaylord!" The crowd applauded, but Doris could barely contain her disappointment. She stepped forward miserably, her shoulders slumped. Mr. Monahan handed her a small bouquet of pink roses and instructed her to stand at the front of the platform. Doris looked at him as if that was adding insult to injury.

"The third runner-up is . . . Miss Anne Marie Zweibel." A petite girl with long red hair stepped forward cheerfully. She took her place next to Doris at the front of the platform.

Okay, thought Rissa nervously. *I'm not in, but I'm not out.*

"The second runner-up is . . . Miss Marjorie Johnson." A tall black girl with shoulder-length hair stepped out of the contestant line, smiling. She too received her bouquet and stood next to the others.

"And the first runner-up is, Hemway pool's own junior lifeguard . . . Miss Rissa Lupinski." Rissa came forward. Mr. Monahan handed her a bouquet of roses that was larger than the others and placed a small rhinestone tiara on her head. She could hear her friends and family cheering wildly. She saw her father and Mary on their feet, clapping. Tears filled her eyes. She didn't mind not winning, she felt so good having all these people there for her.

"Now, the big moment," announced Mr. Monahan, drawing out the suspense. "The new Junior Miss Hemway Park is . . . Miss Lena Laffleberger."

Lena had to be pushed forward by the girls next to her. She wore a sincere expression that said, "there must be some mistake." Marsha, Sara, Nicky, Jim, Roger, and Mike all screamed themselves hoarse cheering. Above them Lena could hear Tad hooting and shouting.

Lena received a large bouquet of red roses, and a crown of rhinestones was placed on her head.

When the contest was over friends and family of the contestants swarmed around them. Rissa saw Doris stomp off the stage. In minutes, Sara and Marsha were by Rissa's side, hugging her happily.

They turned and saw Tad hugging Lena. She smiled at them brightly and they ran over to her.

"If it was not for you I would not have this honor," she said to them. "I am lucky to have such friends."

"We haven't been such good friends," said Marsha. "We've acted sort of crummy to you."

"No, it was I . . . I—"

"No, it was us," insisted Rissa. "Friends?"

"Friends, friends, the best of friends," cried Lena, delighted. In her enthusiasm, Lena reached out to kiss Rissa. *Wham!* They bumped heads and their crowns stuck together.

"Ouch!" yelled Rissa.

"Still the best of friends?" asked Lena, rubbing her forehead. Rissa looked at her and started to laugh. Sara and Marsha joined her. And then one sound drowned them out.

It was the snorting, happy sound of Lena laughing with them.

SUZANNE WEYN has written several books for children and young adults, including *The Makeover Club*, the Avon Flare prequel to THE MAKEOVER SUMMER. She also teaches a class on "Writing for Young People" at New York University. Suzanne lives in Brooklyn with her husband, William Gonzalez, and their two children.